ROY HUFF

This book is fiction. Historical events have been modified.
Any resemblance to real names, events, persons,
or organizations is purely coincidental.

Cover and formatting by Damonza.com

Copyright © 2023 by Roy Huff
All Rights Reserved.

To download your FREE copy of "Salvation Ship," visit
Roy Huff at https://royhuff.net/salvationship/.

Don't forget to visit the link below for your FREE copy of Salvation Ship:

https://royhuff.net/salvationship/

CONTENTS

Chapter 1 1
Chapter 2 10
Chapter 3 18
Chapter 4 30
Chapter 5 39
Chapter 6 52
Chapter 7 63
Chapter 8 76
Chapter 9 85
Chapter 10 92
Chapter 11 101
Chapter 12 115
Chapter 13 122
Chapter 14 130
Chapter 15 136
Chapter 16 139
Chapter 17 147
Chapter 18 156
Chapter 19 164
Chapter 20 170
Chapter 21 176
Chapter 22 181

Chapter 23..................................186
Chapter 24..................................191
Chapter 25..................................199
Chapter 26..................................209
Chapter 27..................................214
Chapter 28..................................218
Chapter 29..................................222
Chapter 30..................................230
Chapter 31..................................233
Chapter 32..................................238
Chapter 33..................................243
Chapter 34..................................252

CHAPTER 1

Date unknown, time unknown, Cairo, Egypt, Earth 2/Multiverse 732

QUINN SPRINTED ACROSS the scorching dune. A fine dust hung low in the air as a deep rumble echoed across the vast desert. Every so often, one of his companions raced alongside him but then lost pace as they strode forward.

An energy bolt grazed Quinn's right arm, singeing his fine hair. Adrenaline surged throughout his body. He quickened his stride. With each advance, the Great Pyramid grew larger, its sides younger, and less worn. Sand grains popped in the air, briefly obscuring the view, and then a thunderous roar billowed from behind.

Dr. Green scrambled closer from the outside and huffed, nearly catching up with Quinn. Another discharge whipped past them. Quinn scuttled faster. Several more flashes flew by in quick succession. One final energy ball kissed his left cheek.

Everything on that side went black before sight slowly returned to his left eye. He fluttered his eyelids until his vision focused, stumbling and coughing as he inhaled the dry air. Sand yanked one knee down, but he pushed himself up.

Sweat careened down Dr. Green's face, and his frazzled gray hair flopped. "I don't think we're going to make it," he shouted.

The pyramid once again transfixed Quinn's gaze. He pressed straight ahead, pushing his lungs and legs to the limit. The dry air burned his lungs, and sand glued itself to any available moisture on his already scorched skin.

Quinn's chapped lips split as they opened. "We'll make it," his voice cracked. His parched throat plagued him, but he ignored it and ran faster.

Quinn's group closed in, with Dr. Green the furthest behind, but they were still missing members. Jeremy, Quinn's longtime friend, raced toward him. "Do you think they made it in time?"

A few more quick energy bursts nearly struck them. Quinn forced an awkward turn. His breathing sputtered, and the sprinting made him nauseated. His knees buckled, but he planted each foot in the sand and stamped ahead. "I guess we're about to find out."

"They're almost behind us," Dr. Green shouted.

"Keep running. We'll get there."

Time flew. Air embraced Quinn's skin as the danger dissolved behind him, if only for a moment. As he progressed, the dunes gave way to firmer ground. His knees wobbled, but he soon found solid footing and doubled his gait. The other stragglers ran behind at a distance.

"You mean you hope we'll get there," Dr. Green replied, out of breath and hair flapping. He glanced back at the threat closing the distance, and his face dropped.

A burst of adrenaline shot through Quinn. He scanned his rear. His comrades weren't the only things moving faster. Their demise grew more imminent with each second. Intense dread gripped Quinn once again. *You won't make it*, a thought in his head whispered. He dismissed the feeling and concentrated on scanning the horizon to locate the pyramid, needing to pinpoint its position for the plan to succeed.

Quinn ignored Dr. Green's quip. Instead, he tapped his temple and pressed record with his cortical implant. "This better work," he said, wondering if the rest of his friends would make it in time and if they would outrun what was following them.

Quinn's feet stopped along the blistering sand. He marveled at the Great Pyramid as it eclipsed more of the horizon with each passing second.

The energy blasts from their pursuers continued unabated, but he signaled to his group to slow down as they approached the pyramid's base.

Dr. Green recognized Quinn's cue and made a few adjustments to their equipment and position as the feed started. Laser fire glided past them. "We need your help," Quinn said to the recording.

Quinn dodged more fire and then blacked out.

New York, September 1, 2025, Earth 1/Multiverse 1, Timeline 1

In his study, Quinn sat at his mahogany desk, wrapped in a well-worn leather chair that creaked every time he shifted. His clothing was a disheveled mixture of a half-unbuttoned shirt, a loose tie, and wrinkled trousers.

He rubbed his eyes, unable to identify any information he could gather other than a cry for help from what looked like Giza. With time loops and multiverses, he couldn't be sure of anything. He suspected hidden agendas, yet doubted his counterparts would reach out if travel was impossible. He needed to discover how.

Despite the excitement from the video, his team was exhausted upon return from their prior trip. He also had other equally important things that needed attention, namely, his wife Cameron and the young one they discovered was on the way.

Still, the video held some urgency, but fatigue drained the initial impulse of a hasty rescue, and before long Quinn found himself questioning the idea completely.

Quinn rested and a bit later streamed the video again with fresher eyes. With the few seconds of imagery he viewed, he wasn't sure if those on the other side of the camera had had much time to embed a clue. He hoped he could tease out a hint from the background. If they found a way to help, he didn't want to walk into the fight blind. The recent unreliability of his time-looping ability made him even more hesitant.

Quinn leaned back in his chair and replayed the video again, scrutinizing every pixel of the footage. A shadow flickered in the recording and drew his eye. He zoomed in, analyzing the shape, comparing it to the information he'd gathered during his recent journey to the array that encircled Earth.

He glanced at his notes scattered across the desk. They contained data, equations, and sketches from his recent expedition, all pointing to the unraveling mysteries he'd encountered throughout his time-traveling existence.

A memory from his recent trip flashed through his mind. The array had given him glimpses of other worlds, other timelines, like fleeting shadows just beyond his reach. It had taken him through another universe, one vastly different than his.

The array was an inverse Dyson sphere he'd constructed through hundreds of lifetime-long time loops when he first discovered how to time travel with his mind. Its creation saved humanity, and it also changed everything in innumerable ways. He wondered if the video's storage mechanism on the array might be the best way to track its origin.

The next day, Quinn and his crew returned to the array segment they called Tier 1, which was now repaired and in its corrected position after a recent sabotage attempt.

The metallic odor coming from the corridors reminded him of his near-death escape, which was still very fresh in his mind. Despite the potential catastrophe from the prior departure, the crew gained video evidence of potential future timelines.

Shortly after returning home, Quinn quickly adjusted and remembered a crucial task he'd almost overlooked. He spent the next ten minutes scanning more stored footage of recent events until he was satisfied they were in the correct timeline and universe.

The process brought back memories of his first few time loops in Manhattan when he reviewed his past in his first life with Cameron. He could even smell the fresh bagels near his old apartment at the time of the search. He'd give just about anything for one of those bagels. Unfortunately, the shop that made them went bust shortly after word of the supernova got out.

There were more variations to consider this time. Quinn's

team studied the video of Egypt again. They questioned all their assumptions but soon agreed on a few basic points. *Someone* obviously sent it. Whether that was himself in the future or a different Quinn entirely, he had no idea. There was no obvious reason to doubt the authenticity of the video, but Quinn thought if they dug more into the images, their work might unveil a few more clues.

Jeremy cut into their discussions. "Am I the only one who thinks this might just be a stupid idea? We barely made it in one piece. Maybe we should reconsider jumping off to some random place just to save another version of us out of God knows how many. Are we going to go gallivanting off every time we watch another one of these videos like we're in some bad sci-fi TV episode?"

"You better not say it," Quinn replied as he eyed Jeremy. Quinn knew which series he was about to blaspheme. Jeremy's face told Quinn he'd decided to keep it to himself.

Cameron stood in the doorway. She wore a loose, earth-toned blouse that draped elegantly over black leggings. She held her arms crossed with a playful smirk playing on her lips and fixed her gaze on Jeremy. Her eyes narrowed as if she was about to tease him for the use of the word *gallivanting* but then softened as the truth of his words sank in.

"I don't think we've decided anything yet. I think it would be a good idea just to see if we can find out when and where this is and if we can go there. For all we know, there might come a time when we need to send a similar message to find a way home," Cameron said.

Jeremy stood slightly apart from the group, arms crossed. He wore dark jeans and a rugged jacket, slightly frayed. "And do you think it's going to be us who saves us? That doesn't make much sense. We can't meet ourselves, can we?" he asked, his shoulders now squared and feet planted firmly.

"Cameron's right. We might not always have this array or one of the outfitted ships with us. We need to learn what we can while we can. We can decide if we plan to do anything about it later, although I'd be lying if I said a trip to the Great Pyramid wasn't on my bucket list," Quinn paused, then added, "And, no. We can't meet ourselves, not technically, but we can meet different versions of ourselves, some almost identical with just a few variations."

Quinn left out a couple of important details about the time-travel theory he was still considering.

"If that's even what or where that is," Jeremy replied.

After the return home, Quinn's team had scoured the infinite number of video messages from other versions of himself in different situations. Some issued warnings, but most were devoid of useful information, at least at first glance. But of the videos they'd scoured, he'd never seen such a direct plea from his crew and from a moment in their immediate future. He deduced that primarily from some of their clothing and accessories.

Quinn increasingly felt the urgency to act. Though his crew seemed fine now, a nagging feeling told him otherwise. But as the moments passed, he reflected on what Jeremy had said. This could be one of an infinite number of versions of the same situation in the same place but in a slightly different scenario. They couldn't save everyone even if they tried.

In an adjacent section of the array, while Quinn and a few others kept accessing the digital video cache and storage area, another crew member, Waverly, focused her efforts on the orbs. During their last journey, she gained firsthand insight into the orb's capabilities by hacking into an evil Quinn's computer. Much of it was still guesswork, but she at least had a few facts and theories to potentially pinpoint a location in the multiverse using only digital signals.

For the last hour, she'd been fumbling with one of the orb containers and watching the playback from her cortical implant on her holo-screen. Quinn had taken the orbs out and placed them in a secure area a while ago, but faded memories of her encounter with the computer systems in the alternate universe kept resurfacing in her thoughts.

Quinn strutted in and spotted the container on the table. "You want to join the rest of us? The conversation is just getting good."

The expression and lines on Waverly's face hinted at many untold stories, which Quinn found intriguing. Quinn pulled up a chair and sat down beside her, exhaling.

He sat quietly and let her play the images on the holo-projected in front of her. When the image of the spheres appeared, he eyed the sphere container resting on the table next to them and slid his hand inside. His fingers encountered a distinct groove encircling the rim and base. He wrinkled his face and then felt again. "Feel that?" he said.

Waverly was hesitant at first, but then slipped her hand in and palmed the sides all the way around.

She squinted. "Yeah, I do. You think it means something? You look like you think you might have an idea."

Quinn's brow furrowed. He hesitated to share his thoughts, especially with Waverly. Although she had been central to understanding the orbs and array-time-travel, he suspected she might be harboring some secrets.

She kept to herself most of the time but always appeared keenly aware of her surroundings. Quinn used to be a loner himself in his awkward stage, but awareness didn't come till later. To succeed, Quinn needed to trust her, especially since she shared the orb discovery instead of hiding it. Ironically, he trusted her more when he knew less about her.

Things had changed as their last adventure progressed, and more questions than answers revealed themselves on their journey home, many of which he didn't realize until he had more time to process what had happened. But there were nagging blanks left to fill regarding how the computer systems accessed her mind using the cortical implants and how they all might be susceptible.

"Not a clue," Quinn replied in a delayed response.

CHAPTER 2

A WHILE LATER, Quinn returned to the video cache. A few people were replaying the video again for the hundredth time, engrossed like it was the first.

"Find anything useful?" Quinn asked.

"Same old, same old. Just what appears to be us. Still can't tell if they're in a different universe or just a version of our current selves set in the future. The fact he's contacting us for help suggests he couldn't loop within his timeline."

"Why not both?" Dr. Green interrupted.

Quinn's eyes widened. He wondered why the other version of himself needed his help and how it might benefit his current world. He kept telling himself, just like there are an infinite number of universes, so are there infinite multiverses. This might be one of those. If so, it meant it wasn't a future version of himself. At least, that was his reasoning.

And Cameron was correct. Quinn could time travel by sleeping and thinking of a desired day. This ability, linked to the holographic universe and dark matter, was shared only by a few exposed to the same material under similar conditions.

The problem was mental time travel wasn't always

reliable. Enough of the particles needed to be present for the trip to occur, so there was always the possibility he wouldn't be able to loop or he wouldn't be able to return to his point of origin when he did.

Quinn's later discovery of the orbs changed things and allowed direct travel between similar universes, but he hadn't worked out all the details of what would happen if he used both methods. Not to mention how they might be involved in stopping, slowing, or speeding up time as Quinn had sort of experienced on the other Earth he'd recently visited.

The infamous organization known as The Way created the orbs, but the origin and function of the tech were still a bit of a mystery. He'd found a chamber on the last adventure on an alternate Earth. He'd gleaned some details surrounding different types of temporal orb travel, but he hadn't deciphered all the details. What they did learn allowed them to pinpoint certain worlds within their multiverse, but those were limited to certain constraints. He could plug those locations into the array and create a wormhole to that location.

"Let's just assume that we want to go wherever or whenever this is. I still don't know how to get there," Quinn said.

Dr. Green attempted a dramatic pause in the hopes of increasing the suspense in the room, but everyone just stared at him until he eventually gave up and unraveled a scroll he'd obtained from a library in Upstate New York. After Quinn's first encounter with time travel, Dr. Green searched in parallel for any historical record of temporal displacement.

Every time Quinn gained knowledge in past time loops, Dr. Green adapted once he knew. Most information Quinn gathered was bogus or unhelpful. But a few consistent pieces emerged. Over time, Dr. Green formed a framework about how The Way might operate.

The most useful bits of intel were the astronomical occurrences that coincided with galactic events like supernovas and other phenomena suspected of channeling dark matter and neutrino swarms in Earth's direction. Quinn only needed a little to allow his holographic mind to mentally travel within his lifetime. They needed a lot more to power the spheres, tech which was still very much a mystery and high on his list of priorities to crack.

The good news was that on their last trip to the alternate Earth, they discovered that the very array Quinn had created could generate exotic matter to form wormholes. That gave them three types of time travel to use if they mastered it. Quinn could use his mental time travel, the array, and the spheres. Understanding the spheres appeared to be the key to mastering all three. Only the array and the spheres would benefit the team since they couldn't ride with Quinn's mind into different timelines.

Dr. Green unrolled the scroll flat on the table. The parchment held its form, surprisingly well-preserved yet rough to the touch. Golden embossed hieroglyphs decorated the treated papyrus. Its tan background contrasted with the gold. Fanciful spheres and pyramids, undoubtedly inspired by the ancient Egyptian culture, lined the edges of its fibers.

The symmetry of the design suggested a careful and deliberate hand in their creation. Quinn imagined the artisans at work, arranging each element until the perfectly balanced shapes told a story.

Dr. Green hovered his hands over the messages as if he were about to touch them, but never did. "Remember what you said your future self told you from one of the digital files we retrieved?"

Quinn ran his fingertip along the edges. "You think this document can tell us more than what we learned from the alternate array?"

"I do. And more importantly, I trust it more. Call me a cynic, but I'm skeptical about the ideas that system forced in her head. Maybe it's all true, but a healthy bit of skepticism goes a long way."

Dr. Green explained some of the details on the parchment and what he thought it meant, along with a few missing pieces of information he was still working out.

"It matches up so far with what we found on the surface, the room I accessed."

"True, but that could be by intent," Dr. Green replied.

Quinn understood that The Way excelled at spreading disinformation to seed chaos through timelines. His team suspected they aimed to foster cynicism, obscuring the truth even when apparent. Quinn grappled with fully countering this tactic and questioned its feasibility.

"And how can you be so sure this manuscript is more reliable?"

Dr. Green gently pulled the parchment taut from both sides and then pointed to a few intersecting lines that juxtaposed the Great Pyramid and Egyptian characters holding small spheres.

"I can't, but two pieces of data are more conclusive together than by themselves. Now back to what that other version of yourself from the future said in the new video archive."

When Quinn and his team found the archive initially,

they found dozens of videos with different versions of Quinn that contained explicit intel about The Way's organization. It also displayed bits and pieces of information about time travel, multiverse travel, and the technology surrounding the orbs, along with general information about the nature of the universe.

Much of the info was coded or incomplete. Other pieces of info they thought might be in code, and even more conflicted with itself. Since their return, they had little time to parse through it.

Quinn squinted, inspecting the message that Dr. Green assumed he understood. "You mean not just a Quinn for every timeline, but a Quinn for every multiverse?"

"Yes. Exactly."

Dr. Green traced several lines on the papyrus, each a different color. Quinn understood the holographic mind version of time travel, which allowed his conscious mind to travel within his body in his lifetime, but intersecting lines represented mechanistic time travel, not in a parallel universe, but a parallel multiverse.

Quinn always pondered the fate of the original mind's awareness when he time-traveled. The scroll imagery hinted at the possibilities for that consciousness.

If the multiverse is like an infinite pot of boiling water with each bubble being a parallel universe, then another multiverse would be like a separate pot of boiling water. There would be no issues with causality or a grandfather paradox if one found a way to hop pots and the orbs would allow them to do that, *in theory*.

They would need to test the infinite multiverse hypothesis first. As far as they knew, they'd only jumped through parallel universes within a single multiverse. Quinn and a select few others could do it with their minds, but the orbs allowed all of them to do it with their physical body and anything else they brought with them.

The orbs suggested a method to traverse alternate multiverses, potentially revealing various pasts or futures without altering their reality.

Dark matter was largely responsible for Quinn's prior mental time travel, and exotic matter allowed for travel between universes through a wormhole. The orbs used a similar mechanism that, in principle, could allow them to travel between multiverses and interact with themselves.

Quinn considered his actions as if he were the other Quinn in Egypt, but without the precise time and location, understanding eluded him. Despite analyzing the video, they remained clueless. Quinn questioned if the problem was even theirs. Speculating about the coordination and origin of their findings made his brain hurt.

"You think your scroll can help us?" Quinn asked.

"I'm sure it's already helped us in some other universe. But this is from Ancient Egypt and deals directly with the spheres. The glyphs on the top appear to be the key to decoding a cipher, a message deeper than the surface meaning the images depict. From what I'm seeing, I think we can use the signatures of each video to isolate a direction to a specific universe and multiverse. The spheres will guide us to the right multiverse and the array to the right universe."

"How can you be so sure?" Quinn asked.

"There's three repeating numbers: seven, three, and two. Those are represented by the glyphs here," he said, pointing. "And if you noticed, there are repeating intervals in the spaces on each line," he said and then went on to explain additional clues embedded in the papyrus.

Dr. Green paused for a moment and then jumped up. "I think I might know how to find what you're looking for. But it might require something special."

He gave Quinn a familiar look. "You think that's such a great idea?" Quinn asked.

"If you want to do this thing and discover what it means, I don't think we have much of a choice," he said, pausing, "or time, for that matter. You can use your implants to speed up the process, but each activation attempt will take time, more than we have if you take this journey."

Quinn could loop time to sort through the footage and follow any other technical analysis each time, comparing a few decoded scroll hieroglyphics and cross-referencing them to the background images in the video. He could also review the captured video from the Ghost Array they found surrounding another parallel Earth to find clues about the orbs.

Dr. Green interrupted, "Unless we can jump both into the past and into another multiverse at the same time, which just might be possible."

Quinn hadn't even considered how to combine time travel with multiverse travel. That would depend entirely on the spheres. And assuming they made it, he wondered if he could still use his mental time travel in a different multiverse. In the prior adventure, he couldn't loop to before they entered the new universe, and he thought it likely that would hold true if they decided to leave.

Quinn, Dr. Green, and the rest of the primary crew spent the better part of the day discussing the possibilities and analyzing the video for possible clues before returning home.

The risk Quinn took when looping was running out of juice and getting stranded. A short loop a day or two wouldn't be that big of a deal, but he was more concerned about running out when he needed to use it the most.

From what he'd gathered from the scrolls, they suggested that time itself was a critical component of how much of the dark matter was consumed with each loop. A shorter loop was much smaller. The number of particles consumed was an inverse square like gravity. What he hadn't determined was the starting point. All he knew was that the total amount of dark matter used grew exponentially the farther in time his mind went. So he decided to travel short hops, a single day.

CHAPTER 3

Date unknown, Cairo, Egypt, Earth 2/Multiverse 732

ALTERNATE QUINN AWOKE flat on the desert sand, and the rest of the group hovered over him. His head throbbed, and his ears rang like he had a bad case of tinnitus.

"What happened?" Quinn muttered.

"You got a glancing blow to the back of the head. You're lucky you're still alive," Cameron replied.

The sound of shaking and low-pitched murmurs rumbled in the distance.

Quinn eased himself into a sitting position. Cameron and Jeremy helped him up. "Where are we?" he asked.

Quinn attempted to stand but quickly stumbled before gathering his bearings one final time.

"We're on the other side of the pyramid, but they'll spot us soon. We threw up a micro dust storm with a few of the tools we have, but it's fading fast and its range is limited," Dr. Green replied.

Quinn rose and traced his hand along the pyramid's

surface. At first, it looked like he was using the side for support, but soon the motion became more deliberate.

"We need to find the entrance," Quinn said, scanning the structure for any sign of a way in. Jeremy and another member of the group finally caught up and then ran ahead, checking for a way in.

Quinn gave a brief explanation of their current situation to the recording and used his cortical implant commands to complete the message and integrate them with the enhanced features from their equipment, hoping another version of himself would find the plea for help and come to their rescue. He knew the odds were slim. And in the likely scenario it failed, he now had to go on to plan C, seeing as plan A failed from the moment they arrived.

A few moments later, Jeremy waved his hands in the distance, barely noticeable. Quinn and Dr. Green packed up the enhancer and sprinted toward him, followed closely by the others, who had all caught up.

They arrived at Jeremy's position, and an entrance barely large enough for one person came into view. "Get in," Quinn said, glancing at their pursuers. He motioned for them to cram inside. A rush of energy surged through him and renewed some of his lost strength.

Just as they squeezed through the narrow opening, an energy bolt slipped through and skimmed Jeremy's cheek.

"Seal it up," Quinn shouted.

Jeremy pulled out a small satchel filled with designer resin. It hardened and set instantly when exposed to the air, making it nearly impenetrable, which meant that they'd need to find a new way out.

Once inside, only a few torches illuminated the pyramid's

dimly lit interior. Quinn's heart hammered away as they ventured further and he breathed in the scent of ancient stone. The deeper they descended into its base, the more he sensed something lurking in the shadows, like eyes spying in the dark.

Thanks to the floor plans in their cortical implants, they avoided getting lost. Quinn closely monitored the identified entrances and exits, pinpointed after their failed attempt. However, the plans weren't precise, with several discrepancies and secret passages at the pyramid's base.

They meandered further inside the labyrinthine structure, exploring for hours and hoping their pursuers would eventually give up and turn away. Eventually, they stumbled upon a hallway containing a few ancient pedestals, where they took the time for a brief rest.

Twenty minutes later, Jeremy inspected the nearby walls. "Another dead end," he said.

Quinn analyzed the plans on his holo-screen and the error. "Maybe this section was sealed off for a reason. There could be a room inside. This pathway should lead to four other locations. That means there's enough space for an enclosed room. If it's here, we could loop around each of the other three sections. One of them might be an entrance. Let's see if we can find anything."

In the pyramid's dim corridor, flickering torches cast elongating shadows on the walls and made the hieroglyph-covered stones appear alive.

A faint rustling whispered from the very depths of the pyramid, a sound that was neither the wind nor the breath of Quinn's companions. "Does anyone else think we're being watched?" Jeremy asked.

"Maybe it's from the same people who lit the torches," Dr. Green added.

"Where are those people anyway? Nobody said anything about torches, or people living here. I thought these were supposed to be tombs?" Jeremy said.

Quinn strained his eyes, searching for any sign of movement but only saw shadow dances. Every so often, a scarab's rustling broke the silence.

Suddenly, one of the torches blew out and plunged the group into near darkness before their cortical implants activated night vision. And for some reason, the temperature plummeted. Quinn shuddered and realized just how deep they were and how little they knew about the structure.

One of them lit another torch from the embers. They continued their descent, and the walls became more elaborate, covered in hieroglyphs and carvings. Quinn ran his hand over the rough surface, feeling the grooves and contours of the coarse limestone.

They arrived at a large chamber at the base of the pyramid. Intricate Ancient Egyptian carvings covered the walls and matched symmetrically to emphasize the placement of the sarcophagus in the center of the room.

The dark, polished stone that absorbed the ambient light made it appear almost black. Complex shapes decorated the polished obsidian lid.

They drew closer, and a faint glint emerged nearby, accompanied by a soft buzzing sound coming from within.

"Should we open it?" Jeremy asked, inching closer.

"I'm not sure that's such a good idea," Dr. Green said.

"We keep looking for what we came for. Try not to get distracted," Quinn replied.

"But it's beaming. That means something, right? Are we just going to ignore it?"

"This is not what we came for. It's either a protection, a trap, or something else we don't need," Dr. Green added.

"He's right. This doesn't match what we're looking for. We move forward. We'll know it when we see it," Quinn said.

Jeremy frowned. "Fine. Let's find this thing then."

They left the sarcophagus and continued their journey using the few clues embedded in their cortical implants overlaid on their existing floor plan. Most of the locations matched up, but Quinn wondered if whoever had designed it had anticipated them being there searching for what they'd come for.

Quinn knew about boobie traps to protect treasure buried with pharaohs, so he wasn't surprised they'd find the unexpected. Dr. Green even warned him of that before they arrived. Quinn kept a close eye on the clues, still not sure how they might appear in real life should they come upon them.

The group continued searching for roughly twenty minutes until they found an easily missed narrow passageway at the heart of the pyramid. It opened to a room fifteen yards across on all sides. A pedestal lay in the center of the room. Resting on top sat a small, flickering orb. Warmth radiated from it.

"That looks like it," Jeremy said, reaching out to take it.

Quinn cut in. "Wait, we . . ." Before he could finish, a low, primal growl arose from the darkness, followed by the soft scrape of scales against stone.

A creature emerged from the shadows. Its eyes gleamed yellow and orange as if possessed. Its claws glinted in the dim torchlight, but the darkness still hid the rest of its features.

The scent that accompanied the creature was equally disturbing, a mix of damp earth, decay, and something metallic and tangy, like the smell of fresh blood. The overpowering stench filled the room.

The animal snarled. The beast easily stood ten feet tall, with scales covering its body, like a snake-cat hybrid. Its long tail whipped back and forth behind it, and its humongous jaws opened and closed, revealing rows of razor-sharp teeth.

Sweat beaded on Jeremy's forehead. He stumbled, almost dropping the orb in his hand, but retrieved it just before it touched the floor. The rest of the team drew their weapons. Quinn quickly spun his head, looking for any advantage they could use. Pillars supported the ceiling, and the encircling creature blocked the only exit.

"Get its attention on one side of the room, and then we make a run for it on the other," Quinn said.

The team said nothing, just quickly split up and took positions behind the pillars. Jeremy stepped forward, holding the orb. "Hey, you ugly thing," he yelled, waving the orb as his heart raced. "Come and get me!"

Jeremy's stomach sank the moment the words left his mouth. The creature crept toward him, its eyes locked on the sphere. It inched closer toward him in slow, deliberate, silent steps.

The team made their way toward the other side of the room. Once they were completely on the other side, the creature lunged toward him, its massive claws extended out to grab the orb. Before the beast could reach Jeremy, Quinn threw a large stone and hit it squarely in the noggin. Its head flicked back, and then it let out a deafening roar. The rest of the team sprinted toward the exit. Jeremy quickly caught up, the strange cat now focused on Quinn.

The creature's footsteps pounded behind them as they

ran. In one giant leap, the beast landed behind them, now forcing them to turn in the other direction.

"Why does this keep happening to us?" Jeremy said.

"If not us, then who?" Quinn asked.

"How the hell should I know? Anyone but us. That works for me."

As they chatted, Dr. Green stood ready to act, though Quinn wasn't sure Dr. Green would be able to do much of anything. Cameron stood immobile, moving her eyes busily as she scanned something using her cortical implant.

The creature retreated, paused for a fraction of a second, and then slithered its torso in their direction, stretching itself to double its prior length.

"Cover your ears," Cameron shouted.

Once the team's hands were over them, she tapped her temple and activated a sound grenade from her cortical implant.

The creature's mouth gaped open, trembling. The scene unfolded like a silent movie. It shrunk to its original size, and they dropped their hands.

"Quick. This way," Cameron said. She took a small rod reinforced with exotic matter and punched through a section of the wall opposite the creature's position. They burst through the entrance into the blinding sun-lit desert.

Quinn quickly sealed the entrance behind them, trapping the creature inside. Jeremy hurled, panting. The rest of the group collapsed on the ground, gasping for air, but they were not alone.

September 1, Earth 1/Multiverse 1, loop 4

At the spaceport on the surface, Dr. Green meandered with Quinn in a remote, off-limits area near a patch of deep green weeping willows near the edge of the promenade. Their long, slender branches swayed in the breeze. Their shade muted the deep green grass below. Quinn inhaled a breath of fresh air with hints of freshly mowed grass. A woodsy scent commingled with soil and nearby lilies.

The warmth of the sun hit Quinn's skin as some nightingales and a few other exotic birds chirped their high-pitched melodies. Children laughed and played in the background. For the short time Quinn was there since his crew's recent return, the place drew him in.

The group discussed their options and strolled across a large promenade near a small artificial pond nestled between the trees. Only a single neon orange carp swimming lazily in its cobblestone depths interrupted its clear water.

After several minutes of going into the weeds on time travel and array design, Dr. Green stopped talking.

Quinn's father and Dr. Green were still authority figures despite Quinn's dozens of lives in actual time when factoring in time loops. Old habits.

"So how many loops this time?" Dr. Green asked.

"Just a few, and just a day each, that whole inverse square thing and all."

"I see. And did you find anything useful?"

"I've made some progress deciphering some of the imagery. From what I can tell, each sphere holds a different combination of exotic matter particles. The inside of the orb uses material that captures spent energy in a field. It appears to be the secret of both how they can hold onto the energy with next to no depletion as well as create a connection to different aspects of space-time," Quinn replied.

"And did you discover if we can use it to take us where we want to go?"

"There are a couple of sequences I'm still not certain of. There's still a lot of guesswork here. I think the only way to learn is by trying. I could always loop if things go south, but that won't help you. And what happens if I can't loop back from another multiverse or if I run out of juice when we're there?" Quinn asked, referring to his ability to mentally time travel to his past.

Dr. Green smiled. "Then I guess we'll be stuck in whatever world, in whatever time we find ourselves in. But we do have access to the orbs, so there's a possibility that we could join you."

Quinn waited for a follow-up and then paused to think before speaking when it didn't arrive. "My first instinct is to save these people, but Jeremy brought up a good point. I'm sure there's more than one version of us out there who needs our help. We can't help all of them," he said and then paused. "And what if they're not us? What happens if they're the evil version of us or something worse we haven't even discovered."

Dr. Green squinted. Quinn knew Dr. Green felt the strain of life like everyone else, only more so, like a mental chore that only grew with time. He just had to find more ways to cope with it, and at times, he succeeded. "Did you find more than one video similar to this one?" Dr. Green asked.

"No, nothing like it at all. We have tons of video images from different scenarios, but each one is different. There could be more. We just haven't found any yet. I didn't want to waste too much time searching for more when I needed to decrypt the cipher, but from what I've seen so far, I don't think we're going to find one."

At times, Quinn's thoughts wavered between a sense of urgency and a disinterested detachment, even drifting toward complete nothingness when the challenges felt insurmountable. But like always, eventually he refocused his attention on the potential solutions and let the possibility of failure fade away.

"What about this? Why don't we focus on finding a way to get there first? Maybe the only versions of us we can help are the versions we can find. Maybe we do what we can to help and then follow the breadcrumbs wherever they lead us. If we're going to discover more about The Way and who they are, we have to start somewhere. And this is as good a start as any," Dr. Green replied.

Quinn thought about it. Searching for a way to travel to any world they wanted made sense no matter what. Discovering a way to track the specific point in the multiverse without the array was something they still needed to refine, and just using the orbs would also be necessary, not only if they wanted to help, but also if they wished to return home. That meant they needed to perfect using them first, and they were a long way from fully comprehending orb science.

Quinn wondered how they would ever find their way home if they got lost in the vast expanse of the multiverse. His Earth was a world he didn't want to leave. Over the last decade, he'd managed to change the world by constructing the array. It gave the world hope many thought was lost. In the five years since the supernova powered the array and

Earth averted disaster, Quinn shifted the direction of the human race. At least in the current timeline in the current universe.

Earth was by no means perfect, but losing so many people in the tumult leading up to a galactic event that nearly wiped out mankind shifted the perspective of many, almost as much as miraculously surviving it. Not to mention that the advancement in science, medicine, and space travel after the supernova activated the array had brought the world together in a way many hadn't believed was possible.

The main question was whether Dr. Green's mention of a multiverse within infinite multiverses was accurate. If so, it would add a new layer of complexity in both navigation and potential problems. It also hinted at whether the current peace was sustainable or if troubles lurking in other worlds would find their way to this one.

The array, Earth 1/Multiverse 1, three hours later, loop 4

From a large window, Cameron watched the movement of transport shuttles and larger spaceships engulf the array like a living lung of motion breathing in and out between Earth and itself. The spherical portable node clusters once again decorated the nearby space. Quinn's original array company founded the new organization, and its members worked outside in mostly open space in large shipyards, building several dozen transport ships used to bring people and supplies between outposts built in the inner planets over the last few years.

Cameron rubbed her stomach and inhaled as she stared at Earth's blue sphere, radiant as ever. She tapped her temple and activated the holo-implants to replay the initial video cache discovery from the future. At the same time, she filtered through the flood of emotions she'd experienced the last couple of weeks.

The last thing she wanted was Quinn treating her like a fragile little thing just because she was pregnant, but if she was being honest with herself, she wondered if it might be a better idea to sit out the next adventure even though she wasn't that far along. But like she often did, she found a reason to shelve the feeling. If the version of her in the video had no issue running off to the Great Pyramid, she likely had a good reason.

Something from the initial find got her thinking there might be more to the messages than what they initially uncovered. The hope was to learn more about the organization called The Way, which she suspected might be behind whatever was attacking whichever version of themselves was in the video. And maybe, just maybe, they might find a solution to stop them before they could do more damage to their Earth.

She screened dozens of video loops, and then hundreds. Before she knew it, she'd been there two solid hours and wondered if Quinn might be worried since they'd had lunch plans. She messaged him and kept going.

An hour later, she stopped the feed. She ran through the images again with her holo and rode a transport to the main control room where they'd discovered the original video message.

She flipped through the controls and made a few adjustments. Her heart rate jumped, and then she smiled. She tapped her temple, activating her communications. "Quinn, I think I found something."

CHAPTER 4

The array, Earth 1 orbit, September 1, 2025, 2:05 PM Eastern, loop 4

YELLOW WARNING LIGHTS flashed, followed by a computerized voice: Warning. Impact detected.

"What is it now?" Quinn said.

The comms channel crackled, followed by Jeremy's voice. "Micrometeors. Lots of 'em. Too small to cause damage but just big enough to activate deflection systems. I've alerted my team to take a closer look."

Inside one of the control centers, Quinn focused on the flashing screens in front of him, tracking the trajectory of each micrometeor. Jeremy's voice cut through the tension. "We're getting some interesting readings here."

Quinn's eyebrows shot up. "Care to be a little less vague?"

"We're running scans now. You'll know when I know," Jeremy replied.

"Quinn?" Cameron said.

"That tone in your voice tells me you've got bad news," Quinn said.

"You know me so well, hunny bunny."

"Spit it out then," Quinn replied.

"There's a malfunction in one of the station's critical systems. I can't quite pin down what triggered it, but whatever it is has shut off the antimatter venting system."

"Do what you can to find the problem and fix it. Any chance it's connected to the micrometeor shower or more importantly, why are the meteors able to get through the array's protective barriers at all?"

Cameron pulled up system specs on her control panel. Her eyes toggled between the screens, and her fingers tapped away at the controls as she tried to pinpoint the source of the problem.

Suddenly, the shaking from the array's sudden maneuvering stopped, and the room grew quiet except for the soft hum of the equipment. An occasional beep or chirp from one of the terminals was the only thing breaking the silence.

"I can't tell, and I don't know why that would be the case. The array's shielding should be taking care of the fragments. There's no visible external damage to the array. The proximity alerts may be malfunctioning, causing the venting systems to shut down or reroute."

As she worked, her gaze shifted to the venting system display. Its red warning lights flashed. The sophisticated venting systems separated the antimatter from regular matter using a complex tunnel of magnetized particles. If the system remained offline for too long, it could have catastrophic consequences for the entire array.

Quinn tapped his comms panel. "Jeremy, any update on those readings?"

"Yes. And unfortunately, it's not good. I've scanned the

system, and it appears the supernova explosion from several years ago obliterated numerous uncharted asteroids. The micrometeor stream remained hidden for so long because the remaining fragments were too small for detection and in one of the blind spots."

"Any chance this could be intentional?" Quinn asked.

Jeremy's comm line activated. "I don't think we can rule it out, but I don't see anything specifically that suggests that. And if it were, it wouldn't be that effective with the array able to eliminate the threat pretty easily."

"Double-check those readings. See if you can back test the trajectories to confirm that it came from the supernova explosion," Quinn said, and then paused before adding, "Exactly how far out does it look like the collisions occurred?"

"Just give me one moment," Jeremy replied.

Several more sirens sounded. "We better do something fast. The venting system is jammed. Safety protocols won't let me open them from the console. Someone may need to go in manually," Cameron said.

"How long do we have?" Quinn asked.

"It's hard to get a good reading, but I'd guess between seven and ten minutes before any systems reach critical. Even then, our main concern would be a full shutdown. The array would need to do another full reboot."

Quinn considered the risk. They'd be vulnerable on certain sections of the array, but the ships in the area and the planet itself wouldn't be affected since hundreds of sub-nodes could fill in the gaps for coverage while they rebooted the main array. And that got Quinn thinking about a possible solution.

"Feels like déjà vu. You've got three, then, to figure it

out. I'll notify the crew near the manual interface to be on standby," Quinn replied.

Quinn tapped his holo-console and zoomed in on the micrometeor shower that was peppering the area. As the micrometeors approached the array shielding, dozens bounced off the shields, ricocheting off in all directions like pinballs, leaving trails of glittering dust.

Jeremy interrupted. "I've calculated that most collisions originate from the Kuiper Belt. Fortunately, the array can demolish the fragments, per its design. Despite earlier damage, it won't be a problem. The main concern is the nodes at each junction point. The coverage is thinner than intended. Regulators are struggling to obtain accurate readings. While they can still annihilate targets, malfunctions may disrupt sensor function and halt orbital manufacturing. Safety concerns seem minimal, but the operational impact is significant. It could completely halt orbital plants."

Quinn squinted. "What are our options?"

"Jeremy is right," Cameron interrupted. "The main concern is how the systems are reading the incoming shower. We don't want the deflection grids pointing in the same direction as the antimatter vent chutes. That would give the sensors a heart attack. We need to manually recalibrate each of the nodes. Then, we'll need you to reroute reserve power from non-critical systems to the venting system. It may not need the power. I can't tell because of the malfunction. Either way, it might work."

"Might?" Quinn asked.

"It's my best guess based on the readings I'm seeing."

"We have redundancies built in should both events happen simultaneously," Quinn replied.

"Had. The third-level redundancy was sheared off in the original separation. The guts are there, but it's malfunctioning. Our only option now is the manuals. So if we can't discover what's causing the sensors to malfunction, we'll be stuck with our glorious manual backups," Cameron said.

Quinn wondered if he should've added another layer of redundancies in the system, but then he put it out of his mind before he began to doubt his decision, something he couldn't afford to do. "Do whatcha gotta do," he replied.

"Give me just a few . . . Almost . . . Almost . . . Done." She waited a second and then added, "If it worked, the system should recalibrate in five seconds."

Cameron's face tightened. A few seconds later she exhaled and then smiled.

"That was fast," Quinn said.

"That's why you married me."

"Just one of the many reasons."

Lights streamed into the view screen. Over the next few seconds, the flickers transformed into a torrent of brightness.

"What's going on out there, Jeremy?"

"The array's doing its job. There's been an uptick in the number of micrometeors. I'm seeing several more clusters coming our way."

"How much longer is this going to last?" Quinn asked.

"Based on the trajectories and numbers plotted so far, we're going to be in the thick of it for a few more weeks."

"Weeks?" he said, letting the word hang in the air. "And you're sure this is a result of the supernova and not something else?" Quinn replied.

"Not sure I can say anything's a hundred percent, but the calculations haven't changed since I reviewed them last.

If you want, we could take a stroll around the Kuiper Belt to get a closer look," Jeremy said.

"We don't have time for that now, but let's send one of the portable nodes in that direction and run some readings just in case. Might not help us now, but we'll likely need that data later. And while you're at it, put in an order to recall a few dozen subnodes. I want the entire planet covered for protection just in case the main array's systems malfunction again. And put a few in front of the industrial space plants."

Jeremy pulled up long-range communications on the panel and tapped out a few commands. "I've just sent the order to recall some of those subnodes. They'll be here within the hour."

"Good."

The main control station where Quinn stood shook. "What's our status, Cameron?" he asked.

The comms went silent. A few more shakes, and then everything went white.

Date unknown [a few minutes later], Cairo, Egypt. Earth 2/Multiverse 732

Alternate Quinn pounded on the pyramid base. "It's sealed shut. I can't get in," Quinn said. He tapped his cortical implant, not sure how many seconds he had before it would be too late.

"Maybe you should've left something to wedge the opening in case we needed to re-enter," Jeremy said.

"Nothing we can do about that now. Just find another way to get in while I figure out another plan."

Jeremy took Quinn's place, searching in vain for a hidden entrance while Quinn's brain went into overdrive searching for something to buy them more time. "Ah, there it is," Quinn said.

A thunderous roar bellowed from what sounded like a hundred yards ahead of them. The creatures blocking their path turned toward the screeching sound behind them. Quinn exhaled. "Finally! Follow me," he said.

"What was that?" Cameron asked.

"Subterfuge," Dr. Green cut in.

"It won't keep them busy long, so let's find a way in," Quinn added.

The crew followed Quinn as he ran toward the right side of the pyramid, all still out of breath. "There should be another entrance on the other side. I'm not sure if it's connected to the main chamber, but it may be able to buy us some time if we can find it," he said.

The group fumbled along the foundation, searching in vain for a loose section or crevice. The pyramid's textured surface glistened in the bright sunlight and sparkled outward. The limestone and mortar blocks that composed the pyramid's outer layers were cool to the touch on the shaded side they searched.

"Maybe we've been doing this all wrong," Dr. Green said. He stopped and gazed toward one side of the pyramid and then tapped his implant. A holo-image projected out in front of him, blinking a few times, just like it had for Quinn.

"Won't work. I tried that," Quinn said.

"I know, but these pyramids need to be finessed. They've been interfering with our cortical implants because of the energy they emit. I think if we find the right frequency like two waves canceling each other out, we can get rid of the noise," Dr. Green added.

"We could link the implants together, but we'd need to override the safeguards," Cameron said.

"You know that's too risky. That's how they sent enemy nanites into the array the first time, and that was despite our partition," Quinn replied.

"We don't need to link them. We just need to bring them closer together to increase the ambient energy field around them," Dr. Green said.

"That's brilliant, Dad," Cameron added.

Quinn thought for a moment and reflected on what the future version of himself said. Maybe that was the missing piece of information. "No. We're not going to do that either. But I think I know where you're going."

He shelved that bit of information and planned to revisit it should they ever return to safety.

"Guys," Jeremy interrupted.

"What we can do is . . ."

"Guys!" Jeremy said for the second time.

The group turned, and half a dozen large creatures barreled straight for them, several holding laser pistols.

"Duck!" Quinn shouted.

Jeremy finagled with the pyramid bricks and then fell in.

Quinn tossed a modified grenade a few yards ahead between them and the creatures and then jumped in the opposite direction into the newly opened entrance.

The blast shook the ground, creating tremors they still felt from the inside. The shaking continued until the entrance was covered. Once the noise abated, silence and darkness overtook them. Quinn activated his implant's night vision. Small flickers of light reflected off something moving from the edges of a large inner chamber and swarmed toward them.

"Another close one," Jeremy said.

"It's not over," Quinn said. "If they don't get here soon, we're all screwed."

The rest of the group activated their night vision, revealing a river of scorpions flowing in their direction.

CHAPTER 5

The array, Earth 1/Multiverse 1, September 1, loop 4

QUINN ROSE FROM the floor, suffering from a migraine. His muscles ached everywhere. "Status."

Sirens blared in the background, and it took a few seconds to receive his first response. "It looks worse than it is," Jeremy finally replied over the comms.

"What looks worse?"

"The damage. A containment breach," Jeremy replied.

"How is that possible?"

"It's actually a good thing. One of those tiny controlled burns you built into the system. Looks like the malfunction in the sensors created a deflection grid that damaged one of the tertiary magnets. And the scanners reveal a break in the micrometeor shower."

"I thought you said we'd be in the thick of it for weeks."

"We are, but there's a twelve-hour window or so before the next cluster reaches us, so we've got some time to shore up the systems," Jeremy added.

"And I think I've found a kink in the sensor readings. When

we were repairing the array after our return, several of the panels connected to the vent shaft were installed backward."

Quinn squinted. "That doesn't make sense. They're double-sided, coated with exotic matter."

"True, but one side has slightly more coating. They can function on either side, but what should be the back side, which is there primarily to balance the anti-grav is just shallow enough to create proximity warnings. It's causing the detectors to think we have no functional vent system, so it's rerouting the vented matter into the ejection trajectory as a fail-safe," Cameron replied.

"How many of these controlled explosions are we going to have until then?" Quinn asked.

"I've recalibrated the sensors, so we should be fine. The panels will work just like you designed them to. We're just a victim of those extra precautions you implemented."

"Maybe we should reinstall the panels."

"Yeah. We could, but we don't need to, and if we do, we'll need to reboot the venting system. Once those panels are hard-drilled with the fancy coated bolts, reinstallation becomes a pain. And with the increasing meteor showers after the window closes, it's not the ideal time, especially if we want to take this section of the array someplace anytime soon."

Quinn put the area in question on close-up on the main view screen. He inspected it for a few seconds and reflected on the original design, which was largely his.

The funny thing was, he remembered thinking something similar to what they were experiencing might happen if they didn't redesign them at some point. He also knew the concern was minimal, and he had to work as fast as possible to finish the array before the arrival of the supernova. Worst-case scenario, they'd have a few malfunctioning hypersensitive sensors. But the damage to the array and extensive rebuilding after being nearly ripped apart complicated matters.

He wasn't sorry about it. Quinn knew they needed to deal with the supernova first and then the improved design. That's when the thought occurred to him.

"We don't need to reinstall it. We can overlay it with a separate sheet of exotic matter."

A perplexed look appeared on Cameron's face. "You sure we need to?"

"Probably not. But if we do end up going through a wormhole to some other multiverse, I want to be prepared for the unexpected," Quinn said.

Several of the flashing lights stopped, and the annoying background alarms quieted.

"I'm getting a full sensor reading now. Just give me a second," Cameron said.

"And I'll double-check the impact trajectories and update our projections. I'll keep you posted. I've also got an update on those subnodes. They'll be in place a few minutes earlier. Do you want to put a couple in front of us at the moment?" Jeremy said over the comms.

"Give it a bit more time. The planet needs more protection than we do. And don't pull them from the current batch. Recall a few from the Mars outpost. They should have more than they need," Quinn said.

Quinn exhaled and tightened his fingers before relaxing them. "You mentioned something earlier about something you found?" he asked Cameron.

Cameron stood up from her console. "We've got a few minutes. Let's talk in the viewing room."

Quinn followed. Cameron strolled toward the large window in the viewing room. The vibrant blue and green hues of the planet contrasted against the endless abyss of space. Spacecraft of various sizes and shapes zoomed past each other. In the distance, the familiar shape of the moon hung low near their position, now transformed by the array into a bustling hub of activity.

Since returning, the development of several large starships rapidly advanced. The array's fleeting disappearance also spurred a rush of docking and refueling at the antimatter nodes, alongside the swift completion of other repairs by the crews.

"I've been reviewing some of the images from the event you asked me to. And I've also done some digging on the video archive to see if I could find anything on The Way and their history other than what we already know."

She paused. Quinn stood staring out the window in her silence. "They're worse than we could've possibly imagined. And it all started so innocently."

"What did you find?"

Cameron's face dropped. "They've annihilated entire civilizations as an afterthought. They destroyed more than you can think possible."

Twenty minutes earlier, Tier 1 simulation room, Earth 1, loop 4

Cameron shut off her cortical implant, placed a simulation visor over her eyes, and activated the core system time device.

While the simulator didn't access the cortical implant, which had to be turned off to function, it did piggyback on the hardware, which was a critical design component that allowed the photons in the simulator to accelerate the neurons to near-light speed. The contraption was sleek and put the appearance of all other existing wannabe copycats to shame.

On their last trip, they found a crystal array that enabled them to simulate scenarios of frozen time. Rather than stopping time, it sped up the brain's neural activity to mimic reverse time dilation.

Gamers dreamed of this feature for virtual simulations, but there were limitations. The photons that fired and activated in the brain would slowly lose their targeting trajectory, so it was only possible to use it for a certain amount of time.

Quinn and Dr. Green self-imposed the other limitations as a safeguard against hacking. They were a combination of a non-networked computer core as well as a kill code that anticipated any possible interference an outside network might try to leverage to gain access.

Even with the limitations, the time simulator was badass. All one needed was a list of situations provided by one's thoughts. One simply thought about a scenario and then verbalized the key variables.

With a few tweaks, Quinn modified the existing crystal structure they'd found on a parallel Earth and combined new techniques with the idea he'd borrowed from his physics knowledge of the holographic mind and his mental time travel ability. He wondered if he'd one day be able to expand the tech further but didn't want to push too far before they had a better understanding of all the implications.

Cameron activated the tech by imagining the team discovering how to travel to the world on the video. She then thought of a scenario where The Way found them and they would need to evade them to rescue the other version of themselves.

She stated the variables she thought were most important and then said, "Activate."

Her surroundings shifted. Instead of the visor and a projected image, it was as if she were dropped into the heart of the Egyptian desert at the construction of the Great Pyramid. The simulation was indistinguishable from what she imagined it would be, right down to the dry air and sand flies.

A line of countless workers stretched across endless miles of desert scattered with donkeys, thick rope, and carriages.

She'd deliberately chosen an earlier time among the less probable options. While the video was unclear regarding the era the group arrived in, the spheres made her think The Way might have the ability to travel to any time, provided it was in a separate multiverse.

She stood in the hot sun at least half a kilometer from the nearest shelter. Several workmasters were but a few hundred feet away when one of them finally noticed her.

One of the parameters she'd programmed into the simulation was language translation—an easy feat for her cortical implant for a known language, or at least easy to *hear* in English. *Speaking* was a different matter.

"Hey, you there," a figure shouted off in the distance. She ignored him and bolted in the direction she imagined in the scenario.

She scanned both directions. As she got closer to the entrance of a nearby structure, she panted. Her legs grew heavy, and she fought the urge to hurl. Something wasn't right.

The crew she'd expected to find was notably absent, and only a few of the structures decorated the rear of the pyramid.

"What am I missing?" she said to herself. She was about to exit but stopped herself. "Quinn? Jeremy? Anybody?"

No one replied, but several tall, muscular figures, likely taskmasters, rushed toward her. "What the hell is wrong with this thing?"

The smooth interface she experienced a second ago glitched, but only for a fraction of a second. "That's it. Exit," she said.

Her pulse jumped, and her heart skipped a couple of beats. The image disappeared, and she flipped the visor off her head, breathing heavily.

She tapped a few commands into the partitioned drive and inspected the code. She wasn't nearly as adept as several others in the group, but she knew this code well enough to search for errant commands or some other interference protocols she might've missed.

Cameron spent the next twenty minutes analyzing what might've gone wrong and couldn't find a thing. "Guess I'll have to go to the source," she said to herself.

She hopped on an array tram, which whisked her away to Tier 1's computer core, the same place that held the video cache. She stepped up to the door, and it opened to an empty room, which she found odd. She was certain several members of the main crew would still be scouring the images.

She activated her cortical implant and entered a few security protocols available only to the critical array crew. Seeing as she was married to the designer, she had full access. Several panels at the bottom of a center console popped open, and a small holo-keypad slid out. She reentered another security command and placed her palm in the center. "Access granted," a feminine computer voice said from inside the room.

She stood up, and lines of summary code materialized on a larger holo-terminal. She entered a few commands, and several icons replaced the code. Each image appeared similar to what she remembered from the chamber they'd found on their prior adventure.

Cameron played back the images using her cortical implant to find the one she was searching for. A few moments later, she tapped a green icon. The screen image dissolved, and more code unfolded in its place. She scrolled up, and with the flick of her finger motioned the chosen section to transfer to a small tablet she held in her left hand.

Once she transferred the key sections, she tapped another icon that caught her eye, one she'd seen before but they'd never had the opportunity, or at least *she'd* never had the opportunity, to inspect. But something about the image called to her, so she tapped it.

Her eyes widened. Screen after screen opened on the holo, each corresponding to a date and location. Despite encryption, the data revealed six-dimensional coordinates in more than half of its content. The first four matched what she understood as space-time. She suspected the fifth were coordinates for a specific universe. But the sixth was what got her excited.

She inferred what she could from the report logs. At first, she thought an alternate Quinn wrote them, but the appearance of several images deeper in the document challenged that notion.

What she thought most intriguing were references to

"The Organization." "The Way" was not used explicitly in any of the passages, but she knew what they referred to.

Report 487: They all died. That's what they wanted. It was an ambush. Almost didn't get away from that one. J.P. And P.S. If you're reading this, these aren't my real initials, so don't come and try to find me.

That one made her eyes bulge, but she read through dozens more.

Report 526: I think they suspect someone is watching them. The last two nights, they discovered my location, but I told no one and left no clues. But it wasn't a total loss. I got some juice from where I suspected they might be storing it. I'm coming back for more. J.P.

That was the last one, but unease prompted her to scroll through all the records, and she soon discovered notable data gaps. The omissions could be a link to the earlier six-digit sequence but remained uncertain. Adding two values to each summary's three digits totaled five. She promoted her cortical implant to sequence the report numbers and executed an algorithm to assess their significance. She reread the accounts as the algorithm detector searched.

A few phrases stood out: *They've lost all their humanity.* And: *They killed them all.* Finally: *They're coming for everyone.*

After she captured all the reports, she instructed the code cracker to run in the background, and she returned to the simulator room with the updated code on her tablet.

She noted the glitches came from the missing information and patched in the new code. Upgraded software Quinn developed when constructing the array anticipated merging different computer languages. It incorporated all established conventions and proactively anticipated potential languages for translating future protocols on the fly.

The crystals extracted from the chamber bore traces of various computer languages, underpinned by an entirely alien framework. She suspected that gaps in the simulator arose from the code failing to match with specific sequences during crucial exchanges. Still, it did a tremendous job at interpolating.

"Let's hope this works," she said, scanning the lines of code that unfurled into the main partitioned drive. Miraculously, it functioned.

After checking the updated configuration and adding information she had gathered about The Way into the simulator, she flipped down the visor, manually entered the variables this time, and said, "Activate."

She found herself closer to the pyramid than her last entrance, in a cloud of dust. The simulator had also dropped her decades later, with it fully constructed. A few donkeys rode past her, kicking up the dust cloud even further.

Up ahead, a cluster of people, which she couldn't make out in the distance, hugged the base of the pyramid. She wasn't sure what she'd find if they were the simulator version of those they'd seen in the video.

Cameron jogged toward them, squinting. A few hundred yards closer, Jeremy and Dr. Green became visible. She slowed briefly but soon quickened her step when they waved her down. At first, she thought they were just happy to see her, but when the first blasts of laser fire shot past her, she sprinted toward them.

When she arrived, they ushered her below a small stairwell that led underground below the pyramid's edge.

"You're lucky you're alive. Quinn didn't make it. They got 'em right in the back," Dr. Green said.

"What?" she said. Just then, she saw Quinn's body lying on a slab of concrete stone. For a second, she almost forgot she was just in a simulator, but it still nearly gave her a heart attack.

"I hope he wakes up in the past. He gets a do-over each time he dies. Right?" she said.

"We don't know for sure. We weren't sure if he was already out of juice. He said he did a few loops already. But either way, he's dead in this timeline. Better get used to it."

She doubted her dad would say that in real life and assumed that was the simulator's way of dealing with her father's high-functioning autism.

Cameron found the only place flat enough to sit, but it was still hard and uncomfortable. She exhaled, taking in the surroundings and comparing it to her memory of the images in the video and what she thought the actual place might feel like. She had to admit that it was beyond lifelike. Her memory construction, at least from a sensory standpoint, was perfect. It was the scenario, the important part, she wasn't yet sold on.

"So why are we here?" Cameron asked.

Jeremy lifted his head from Quinn's corpse with tears pooling in the corner of his eyes. He reminded Cameron of a sad puppy dog.

It took a moment for Cameron to notice the group wasn't complete. In the video, a faint image of at least a couple of other companions trailed in the distance and were running ahead of some pursuers.

"Did the others make it?" she added.

"You know why we're here. And as to the others, I'm

afraid they met the same fate as Quinn. We're being hunted," Dr. Green said.

"By The Way?"

"By whoever's guarding what's inside these pyramids, the reason we came here."

"Which is?" Cameron asked.

Dr. Green fumbled around, looking as if he were still deciding what to do next and still not responding.

"Dad. Focus. What did we come here to find?"

"Why are you asking me that? You know why we came here," Dr. Green replied.

"Humor me. Just tell me again."

A loud bang interrupted them, and then another. Sand mixed with fine dirt and silt jostled free from the ceiling and walls. Cameron wrapped her shirt around her mouth and nose.

"This way," Dr. Green said, pointing in the direction of a dark, narrow walkway on the opposite side of the room.

Cameron stumbled, smacking her shins hard into a boulder low to the ground. She grimaced and rubbed her leg.

"Hurry," Dr. Green said.

"So what is this thing we're looking for?" she asked again.

He rushed ahead, and she labored to keep up, mainly due to dodging the stones and sharp edges all around her. She thought his swift pace must also be a function of the system, as was the fading pain in her shins, which normally would linger for a much longer time.

She activated her cortical implant, then remembered she was in the simulation and it wouldn't function as expected. The program would drive the output and not her real implant. She activated it anyway, lighting up the darkness with night vision.

"It's just up ahead," he replied.

She glanced behind her. Jeremy struggled even more, and there was other movement in the chamber they'd just left.

"Someone's inside here."

"That's not unexpected. We are taking what's theirs, after all," Dr. Green replied.

"And what are we taking again?"

"The holy grail."

"Wait. *What?*"

"Not the actual Holy Grail, of course. But our holy grail. The reason we came here. To find what we've been looking for."

"Which you never explained," Cameron replied.

She sighed, something she normally didn't do, but she hated getting the runaround. It reminded her of how her father used to act when she was a young child before he became more adept at pretending to fit in.

Her vision glitched. "Not again."

She kept running, the pain in her leg now replaced with a sharp burning in the center of her back. Suddenly, her motion slowed, like she was walking horizontally through water. She pushed and struggled but to no avail. The air around her rippled, like a distant mirage in the desert.

She tried to speak, but the words didn't come out. She resorted to thinking of the exit command, hoping the simulator could read it.

Quinn had built several safeguards into the simulator, the first one being that it automatically shut off in one second of real-time, but that wasn't much consolation if the neural synapses in your brain were traveling at near-light speeds.

CHAPTER 6

Date unknown, a few minutes later, Cairo, Egypt, Earth 2/Multiverse 732

THE SCORPIONS SWARMED closer to the group, now covering Jeremy's shoes. "Oh crap," Jeremy said. He jumped around, wildly flailing to flick off the few scorpions that crawled onto his shoes. "Do something, guys," he said, still hopping like he was doing a funky dance.

Quinn tapped his temple, and immediately the swarming ceased. The floor lay covered in a thick mat of scorpions nearly motionless, but only for a brief second. In the next moment, the scorpions reversed positions and flowed in the opposite direction.

"What was that?" Jeremy asked.

"A motion pulse. Comes in handy against certain small creatures. Too bad we couldn't use it for our pursuers outside. It doesn't last long, though, and it uses up a lot of energy. Let's just hope we don't face too many more of those," Quinn replied.

Dr. Green projected a green, fluorescent map from his

cortical holo-emitter. "See this room," he said, pointing. "I think what we're looking for is here."

Quinn squinted, attempting to decipher anything he could from the tiny dot on the screen. Growls came from behind them.

"Run!" Dr. Green shouted.

"Anything we can throw at them?" Quinn asked.

"Nothing that will work," he replied.

"Then let's throw what we can," Jeremy said, fumbling through his bag as he ran. Dr. Green tapped his cortical implant, "Nothing in here," he said.

Quinn thought for a moment. "We might not have enough power to stop them, but we could cause a partial collapse of a few nearby structures if we all use the same frequency on the emitter."

"That just might work," Dr. Green replied.

"Alright, you see that small narrow passageway just before the entrance? I'll turn to face the creatures there. We'll target the walls and pray to God it works," he said.

The growls grew louder. Nails from one of the beasts chasing them snagged Jeremy's shirt. "One of them's got me," he shouted, still running.

"It only nicked you. Keep going. Don't look back," Quinn said.

"Why in the hell would I do that? Do you think I'm the kind of person who would look back?"

"You really need me to answer that?" Quinn asked.

Another claw scraped at Jeremy. Quinn yanked him forward while still running ahead.

"Almost there. Let's just hope our duplicates can find us once we've barricaded ourselves in," Dr. Green said.

They approached the narrow corridor where they planned to make their move. "Alright, turn around," Dr. Green said.

"Now," Quinn added.

At that moment, the entire group activated the same frequency. Nothing happened at first, but then a rumbling noise and a cloud of smoke engulfed them.

"Turn around and keep moving," Dr. Green said.

Tier 1 simulator, Earth 1/Multiverse 1, September 1, loop 4

Cameron finally relaxed her body, giving in to the simulation for the moment. She was tired of fighting it and just wanted a little physical relief from the constant tension, especially now that she'd need to devise a way out.

At the moment, her entire body was suspended, frozen in a snapshot of the simulation half a dozen feet behind Jeremy and Dr. Green. She could think and move her eyes and speak, but not much else.

She'd already called out to the simulator version of them but had gotten no response. She'd tried dozens of voice and thought commands with no success. She wondered if the real version of her friends felt the same way on the other side of the video they'd found.

"Why did I even come here?" she said aloud, already knowing the answer to the question. What she meant to say was she should have at least told somebody. Cameron estimated how long she'd be stuck in the simulator until the safety shutoff, but she'd set it shorter for one millisecond.

Given time dilation at the rate of the enhanced neural synapses, she'd already calculated she'd be there for a maximum of one week. Normally, the way time dilation worked, it would be the observer who'd experience a longer time, but the simulator operated by having the person experience a longer time relative to the outside world. It applied a combination of exotic particles and the enhanced crystals they'd collected from the other Earth they'd recently visited.

Over the next several hours, Cameron attempted to become more comfortable being alone with her thoughts. She had to for the sake of her sanity. The first hour was the worst, but she soon settled into a pattern of alternating between a few minutes of mindfulness meditation, reflecting on her future motherhood, and planning for different scenarios in both the real and virtual worlds when confronting obstacles.

She struggled to grasp the simulator's concept, even more than her cortical implant. Despite warnings, deadlines and a formidable enemy manipulating time forced them to cut corners. She hoped these shortcuts wouldn't prove fatal as they tried to stay ahead of their pursuers. She just wished someone was with her who would be a heck of a lot more capable with any computer system, like Sam or even Gary.

Cameron thought they would likely have similar problems, but maybe not enough to get mentally trapped in a simulator.

After a few more hours, Cameron had cataloged several different strategies she planned to implement as a parent. She knew most of them would likely get thrown out the window once the baby was born, but she needed to do something to keep her mind from going into a negative spiral.

The mindfulness meditation helped more than she expected. Soon, she seamlessly shifted between pondering how to reactivate the simulator and contemplating actions if they found their alternate selves in a version of Egypt.

Around the five-hour mark, a subtle change in the surroundings sparked Cameron's curiosity. It was as if a faint light radiated in a rhythmic pattern in her visual field, and then something occurred to her.

The most noticeable changes came after meditation. She theorized it might be changing her brainwave patterns in a way that allowed her to access or at least better sync with the simulator's systems. It made sense based on her limited understanding of the technology.

She spent more time meditating. After each session, her memory became easier to access. And with each thought she retrieved, she captured a crisper snapshot of that moment in time. Her neurons synced with what her conscious and subconscious mind wanted to access.

"Ah, took you long enough," a voice said.

Cameron attempted to speak, but her mouth was still immobile.

"Come on. You can do it."

Who are you? Cameron thought.

"Great. You figured it out. As to who I am, well, that's a bit complicated. You can think of me as artificial intelligence, but that's not exactly accurate. I'm more of a memory or an impression left by a real person."

Like an upload from someone's brain?

"Not exactly, but that's closer to the truth than AI. It's more like an amalgam. Bits of me come from a crude copy of a real person from a version of Earth close to yours, one that's diverged over time, of course. And parts come from a sophisticated matrix within the crystals your team brought to the ship from your last trip."

Can you get me unstuck or unfrozen, or whatever this is?

"I'll do one better."

The moment the system communicated those words, Cameron found herself in a small cottage in the French countryside, sitting in front of a small table with a small cup of hot coffee and some sliced cheese. The scent of grapevine flowers wafted in with a fresh breeze through a crosscurrent.

Two windows on either side of the room opened to a vast vineyard with distant mountains somewhere north of the French Alps. On one side, pink flowered vines dangled around the edges of the white stucco window, partly obscuring the view of a magnificent sunset. The other side featured a distant peak in the darkening sky.

A figure materialized, sitting on a simple chair across the table. He appeared to be a man in his fifties or sixties. She couldn't exactly tell. Fine lines decorated his eyes, just enough to make him look seasoned. He wore subdued clothes with an approachable and unintimidating appearance. "So what do you think?"

Cameron smiled. She nibbled the cheese and sipped the coffee. "Good match. Now what can you tell me?"

"I can tell you a lot of things. Care to be a bit more specific?"

"Let's start with explaining yourself a bit more and why you're here."

"Ah, yes. That. Well, I've already explained a bit of what I am. But I'm afraid if I tried to explain any further, you might not fully understand. You see, I've had a peek inside that brain of yours, and even with your cortical implant, it would take too long to explain the rudimentary basics. But as to why, well—" the figure paused "—you activated my systems by depressing your brainwaves. I was designed to have my systems activate when certain conditions within the simulator were met, a safeguard of sorts."

"Since you know what I'm thinking, can you help us?"

"It would be inaccurate to say I completely know what you are thinking, but I do have a general idea."

Cameron resisted the urge to say something snarky and instead inhaled the fresh breeze before speaking. "Then can you give me a general idea of how you can help us?"

"You'll need to be more specific."

"A few things. Can you get me out of here?"

"That's a cinch. Whenever you're ready, say the word, and I'll have you out of here in a jiffy."

"Great. I guess the next thing is whether you have thoughts on the video of our alternate selves. Should we go, and if we do, can you help us?"

"Help you do what exactly?"

"Help us get there, help them, and get home."

"I'm not all-powerful, and I live within this construct. My help would be limited to you and those who can access me, and only within the construct."

Cameron got a sense he might be withholding something but didn't want to dwell on that possibility, seeing as the AI, or whatever he called himself, could interpret her thoughts. Still, she knew Quinn interacted with the construct during their prior adventure, so she had more trust in it than she would otherwise.

"Is that a yes? Do you know a way to locate the exact time, space, and point within the multiverse where this was taken? I'm not even clear on when this was taken or what time it would be there should we arrive."

"Ah. That's the easy part. I do have access to all the

information connected to the construct, but nothing on the outside. Fortunately, the video archive you are referring to is part of that archive. But I haven't taken the time to analyze it since someone added it later. What I don't have access to is any outside networks or systems. That was by design. So I may need some additional context to give you any possibilities."

"How much of the environment within the construct are you controlling?"

"I'm simply drawing from several prominent images within your mind. And while I don't have access to everything within that noggin of yours, what I do have is a very specific set of algorithms designed to elicit certain responses for a host of circumstances. This one is easy."

"And what about everything else?" Cameron asked.

"You can think of me as a former human's memory with a cyborg mind who has access to a very sophisticated computer bank and certain related peripheral systems. And partial access to anyone who jacks into the simulator. But that last part has additional limitations. What I'm *not* is a magician, an all-powerful AI, or some omniscient being who can traverse time. I can only go wherever the crystals go. I can only control certain aspects of the simulator and those jacked in. At least for the time being."

"Can you talk to anyone outside the simulator?"

"In theory, it might be possible to create an interface using the crystals within a certain radius of the restricted core you brought, but the construct has certain hard limitations. That's part of the reason this is the first time I've been able to contact anyone from your party since you've returned home. I had to wait until you repaired Tier 1 and the array sufficiently, so all the computer systems and infected areas were repaired and sealed off. Those who designed me didn't want certain people to access my information."

The AI was referring to the initial hijacking attempt of Tier 1 and the adventure that ensued as Quinn and his team did what they could to stop it.

"Tell me more about how well you can read my thoughts," Cameron said.

"How about I show you," the construct said.

The French cottage transformed into a computer matrix mixed with a neural net and fuzzy playback of her memories.

"Hold on a moment. Let me give you full access. You'll see what I see and will control what I can control, but only for your mind. Due to security measures, I can't share with you any other minds."

A whooshing sensation overcame her, and the matrix expanded a thousandfold.

"If you want to zoom in, you have to feel it and think about it at the same time. Sometimes it helps if you hold your phantom hand out and zoom in like you're using a touch screen. Play around with it a bit, and you'll get the hang of it pretty quickly."

Cameron toggled from memory to memory. She opened dozens of them, a few personal but nothing she'd be embarrassed about. The ones she'd walled off and kept to herself, she was unable to access. She was, however, able to retrieve more than she could in her normal waking state, but they needed to be somewhat close to the surface.

After several minutes of trying to recover lost thoughts before her earliest childhood memory, she was satisfied the construct wouldn't be too invasive. At the same time, she was a little disappointed that its functionality might not be able to help them as much as she'd hoped. Still, she'd take any advantage she could get.

"What's your honest opinion? Should we try to visit the place in the video? And if we do, what are our chances?"

"If I were in a bad novel, I'd probably sigh right about now."

Cameron smiled. She appreciated the sense of humor but also hoped her emerging trust wasn't misplaced.

"Exactly how many minds have you interacted with?"

There was a brief pause. "That depends on how you define interaction. From my database, I've come in *cursory contact*, defined as those who've plugged into the new system, with about seventeen people. Those are all from Tier 1. But you are the first person who successfully fully activated my program since your return home."

"Are you able to access someone's mind even if they don't activate your program?"

"On a much more superficial level. I can only read what's stored on the database of the simulator, which pulls from a more restricted set of memories."

"And what about before? How many more people's memories can you access?"

"Before your return home, my system only had close access to two other people. But it had cursory access to several hundred people and even a few dozen animals."

"Animals?"

"Yes. It appears in the early phase of my testing, I was connected to several canines and felines, a few apes, and even a couple of mice."

"And all this information is stored in your database?" Cameron asked.

"Yes. The crystal cluster Quinn pulled from the planet contains all of that, along with all the information originally uploaded from three different versions of your Earth and limited external information on several hundred more. My memory database is extensive, and while it's not unlimited, for almost all purposes it's practically so. I'm able to compress the data via the crystals using a substrate of exotic particles that allows me to offload material temporarily should my storage capacity exceed an undefined hard limit. Beyond that amount, info can be stored, but pulling the data requires me to migrate other records. It also slows my processing speed when I do. The good news is that it takes some time for that practical limit to be reached."

"So what can you tell me about The Way?"

CHAPTER 7

The array, Earth 1 orbit, September 1, 2025, sometime later, loop 4

OVER THE NEXT couple of hours, Quinn and Jeremy assigned the best programmers available to create an interface that would allow Quinn to tap into the construct. One option required him to plug into a tapered version of the simulator, without all the bells and whistles. A potential problem was that it took a few minutes to access, which would prove less useful in urgent high-stakes situations.

The second access option was near instantaneous but limited to summaries in a glorified search function. Still, Quinn thought both features would prove extremely helpful. The one drawback of the streamlined versions was that they couldn't use the time dilation technique like the full simulator, something related to the safeguards built into the original crystal construct. Quinn thought it didn't matter much since he could always go to the simulator if he needed to access it that way.

As a final test, Quinn logged into the new streamlined access point in the control room, essentially one of the many decentralized bridges across the array. The moment his visor clicked, an image appeared in front of him in a sterile room, one that vaguely reminded Quinn of the holodeck from *Star Trek: The Next Generation*. Sitting on a small chair sat the construct.

Quinn held his hands a foot in front of his face and rotated them, inspecting for any differences between his real-life body. He didn't notice any. He thought that boded well for the technology.

"Glad you could join me. I assume you have some questions?"

"You could say that. I guess we should start with what I should call you," Quinn said.

The construct smiled. "How about Sentry? Has a nice ring to it."

"Sentry it is. Now what can you tell me about the organization known as The Way?"

"Funny you should ask. Cameron had the same question."

Over the next ten minutes, Sentry explained all he knew. Quinn recognized the initial bits, mentioning The Way's belief in spreading chaos to converge worlds. Quinn didn't quite follow all the logic, but as Sentry explained further, it became clear that they had no set of morals other than survival.

Sentry told Quinn about all the different interactions with people who work with and for The Way. Many of them didn't know the parent organization pulling their strings, and some of the groups shocked Quinn, well-known nonprofits whose mission statements professed peace and prosperity.

Quinn suspected many people who worked with them, especially mid- and lower-level workers and volunteers, were clueless and well-intentioned. That would make it much more difficult to counter potential attempts as they arose.

There was still a lot Quinn didn't know about the network. That included how the organization coordinated time and interdimensional travel and identifying the top leader, if one existed. Quinn also thought it highly likely there were different group iterations and wondered how that worked in practice.

Sentry provided a few bits and pieces that might provide clues, threads that Quinn could pull on should the situation arise. What was clear to Quinn was that The Way would not likely let Earth simply be. He wasn't sure if or when The Way would target his home again, but if he needed help, he hoped some other version of himself would come to his aid if he'd been the one to put out a call for help. It cemented his decision.

A while later at Tier 1's central command center, Quinn gazed straight ahead. "Alright. We go for broke. And if I get into any trouble," he said to Cameron, pausing, "I know what to do."

For the next few minutes, Quinn explained his plan. After he finished, she gently gripped his hand and simply said, "It's worth a shot."

Quinn considered asking Cameron if she wanted to stay back, given the news of her pregnancy, but decided against it. She was a valuable addition to the team, and a version of herself was on the other side of the video too.

The array, Earth 1 orbit, September 1, 2025, 6:00 PM Eastern, loop 4

A muted pop and slight vibrations alerted Quinn to Tier 1's separation from the full array, interrupting his call with Cameron. Quinn huddled over a sturdy container that held several silver orbs, so shiny and clear, they reflected the light perfectly, like a flawless mirror. Quinn thought if birds were nearby, they would knock themselves out, flying into the orbs like a glass window. Another thought came to him of the child robot saboteur he'd seen floating out in space when they'd returned.

Last time, necessity had forced Quinn to separate Tier 1. Now, they were knowingly venturing into danger, risking all who chose to join. Yet, they had to decide, and Quinn wouldn't dismiss the call for help without solid evidence of a trap, which he lacked.

There was also the issue of bringing with them a large section of antimatter storage within the array segment itself. That couldn't be helped. But at least this time, it would be on their terms. Quinn and the crew had enough time to stabilize and activate safeguards for the remainder of the array, and there was plenty of antimatter to go around. Still, Quinn couldn't help but feel like he was playing games with a really expensive toy, at least until they knew why the other versions of themselves needed help. But the new crystal construct gave Quinn some reassurance he didn't have before.

Vibrations shook the room. Quinn's stomach sank, reminding him of his entry through the hole in space. But this was a controlled push, just before the inertial dampeners kicked in. And despite the clean fuel, he could swear a faint scent of an engine filtered in during detachment. He chalked it up to a stronger-than-usual power of suggestion.

Quinn jumped up. His brow tightened. Cameron entered the main control room and grasped for the handle as the array rocked up and down. His crew held positions around the room, and all found their balance. Cameron tapped several translucent keys on the holo-panel. "Here goes nothing," she said.

The orbs rolled in sync with the vibrating sin wave on the holo.

"You sure this is going to work?" Cameron asked.

"Nope," Quinn replied.

"Very reassuring."

"I can try to loop back if things go sideways."

"Won't help me," she said.

That point always troubled Quinn. And even though he always knew each universe would exist anyway, he was still driving the current version. No matter how hard he tried to compartmentalize, it often felt like a guilty death by a thousand cuts.

"Jeremy, any update on the micrometeor shower?" Quinn asked.

"Sensors display a gap in the cluster. No detectable damage. And the remaining section of the array will be fine. It did manage to field off an entire supernova, so I wouldn't worry too much. But I've run checks on all tiers. No reports of damage, and we've added additional integration into sensors to account for the faulty panel designs."

Before they left, Quinn and Jeremy agreed on a twenty-seven-member team for the Tier 1 segment of the array they would take on the trip. It could hold thousands more but was triple what they needed to simply operate the segment with a skeleton crew. They wanted to limit the number of people at risk but have enough for redundancies in case of the unexpected. They also wanted to bring only those already familiar with Quinn's secret, which included a few who learned of it in the prior adventure. Less than half of those knew the true extent of Quinn's ability. Most were only aware of the array's ability to construct a wormhole.

In total, Quinn possessed eight spheres, each slightly different. With the knowledge gained from their prior trip and what they had learned from Sentry, they arranged three of the spheres on a newly created panel connected to the array's navigational system within the central control room, which essentially acted as a bridge for Tier 1.

"Placing sphere one now," Quinn said.

Cameron monitored sensors, and Jeremy inspected navigation on a personal holo-screen in the same room.

"No change in readings yet," Cameron said.

"Placing sphere two now."

Quinn tapped a couple of commands and compared the spheres' placements to the required placement pattern he'd prepared.

Jeremy read his screen. "No changes here either."

"Prepare for activation. Placing sphere three now," Quinn said.

The moment Quinn placed the third sphere on the panel just like the one they'd seen before, they found themselves hurtling toward an alien planet in the not-so-distant past.

Cameron tapped away at her holo-panel and scanned the readouts. "I think it's working."

The room shook violently. "Partial internal dampeners activating now," Jeremy said.

On the main screen, a pitch-black beam erupted from the central node, slicing into the space ahead. The region grew larger until it encompassed half the sky in front of them.

"A wormhole is opening up directly in front of us," Quinn said.

In a microsecond, all the stars disappeared. Total darkness surrounded them.

"I'm not getting any readings on the space around us, but we are moving," Jeremy said.

A chime sounded from the newly constructed panel that allowed the spheres to connect with Tier 1. Cameron activated several controls on the interface. "The panel shows we're traveling through the network multiverses."

"How much longer will it take?" Quinn asked.

"That question is a bit complicated to answer, but from the readings, we should be there in what will feel like a few seconds," Cameron replied.

"And I'm assuming it should be instantaneous relative to our Earth and time of departure."

"That should be the case, but we'll have to wait until we return to confirm that."

A small area of stars emerged on the screen, spreading rapidly until the blackness vanished.

"We're here," Jeremy said.

"Pull up Earth on the viewscreen and see if we can get an image of the surface," Quinn said.

"Done," Jeremy replied. Every continent rested in its correct location. Nothing out of the ordinary stood out from the distant image of Earth.

"Are we picking up any artificial satellites or communications from the planet?" Quinn asked.

"Checking now," Cameron said. Her face remained stoic as she scanned through the readings.

"No satellites are in orbit that I can detect, or anywhere in the solar system, for that matter. There are no communication channels of any kind on the planet except for one single location."

"Let me guess," Quinn said.

"Zooming in for a closer look," Jeremy said.

The view screen displayed a wide angle of the Great Pyramid at the center. All other pyramids appeared there as well, with much less wear than Quinn remembered them having.

"Are we in the right time and place?"

Cameron entered a few commands on the interface. "If these readings are accurate, yes. The images of the surface and the current state of infrastructure support that as well."

"What can you tell me about the reading you're getting from within the Great Pyramid?"

"Not much. The structure itself is partially masking the signal, but I don't see any direct attempt to hide its signature. It matches the frequency we identified from analyzing the video. That's about all I can detect. It's very faint," Cameron said.

Quinn entered some queries into the streamlined interface. "Sentry thinks we're on the right track, and the other version of us is likely somewhere there on the surface in or very near that frequency. The question I have is, if they are, what happened to their ride? I wonder if they may have a ship or an array segment somewhere and are masking the signal."

"My guess is we'll find the other versions of us somewhere inside the Great Pyramid. It makes sense they'd be looking for whatever's causing that frequency. We can ask questions and make guesses, but I don't think we'll find what we're looking for orbiting the planet," Cameron said.

"You're right. But I'd feel more comfortable with you up here. We need someone who can access Sentry, and we'll need someone to swoop in for a rescue if things get dicey. I don't even think we should land the shuttle. Just take us in close and drop us off," Quinn said.

Cameron gave Quinn a glance that said she understood. The other Cameron in the video might be on the ground in the thick of danger, but this one didn't have a problem staying back. She came with the team, and that was risky enough. She would prove invaluable as always, but she could do it at a distance. The chance to swoop in for a last-minute rescue was a bonus.

Quinn initially considered taking everyone who appeared on the video to the surface. Two heads might be better than one, but then he thought they might benefit from each person's expertise. In the end, Quinn decided to bring Waverly, Jeremy, and Dr. Green. One of the flight experts would take them close to the pyramid, and Cameron would be their eyes and ears in the sky.

An hour later, Quinn loaded into one of the small shuttles attached to Tier 1. They had several more, along with a medium-sized starship just in case they needed one. Exotic alloys encased the shuttle itself along with a microantimatter node and backup propellant-powered drive. It was comfortable enough for the entire team, with room to spare. Quinn insisted on a portable med station, and it also contained a food printer as well as backup rations in case the printer malfunctioned.

Flight expert Axel was one of the members Quinn trusted with the time travel secret, parts of it anyway. Quinn had already fully briefed him to have him fly the shuttle. Quinn could've flown it himself, but a flight expert brought additional experience in possible critical situations.

Axel was a seasoned pro. He was tall, muscular, and exactly what one might imagine from an elite military team with special services training. He'd served in active duty before the announcement of the supernova and was one of the first array team members to join when Quinn announced it. Axel had proven himself in every way up until that point, and Quinn had been eager to make him part of the inner circle.

"Scanning flight trajectory now," Axel said.

Jeremy reviewed the life signs readings and surveyed the area near the target drop-off. "System check completed. I see a nice spot where you can offload us without too many spying eyes," Jeremy said.

"I see it. Entering the coordinates into navigation controls now," Axel said.

"Take us in," Quinn said.

Axel tapped on the control panel. "Activating thrusters."

A small screen at the front of the shuttle interior allowed them to follow their descent.

"Partial inertial dampeners active," Jeremy added.

The screen displayed them descending at a steady but brisk pace toward the African continent from a point high above geosynchronous orbit. The initial slow drop was uneventful. They took a cautious approach just in case they found something unexpected.

"Gotta say, I've been dying to go to the pyramids. I know these aren't exactly our pyramids, but close enough. What about you, Boss? Any place in particular you want to go?" Axel asked.

As children, Quinn and Jeremy often dreamed of visiting many places, especially the pyramids, but Quinn caught a scowl creasing Jeremy's brow as Axel spoke.

"Top on my list too. This isn't exactly how I wanted to visit them, but with all the research Dr. Green and I have been doing, I've been itching to go. Let's just hope we get out of this in one piece, and let's plan a proper trip when we return."

"You're on," Axel said.

Having traveled the world as a service member, Axel believed the trip held the promise of an unbeatable adventure.

"Why haven't you gone already?" Jeremy asked.

Axel's face remained unchanged. "I've got no good reason."

A comms message from Tier 1 beeped on the side communications panel on the left side of the shuttle. Quinn tapped the command to open the channel. "There's something . . ." was all Cameron could get out before the shuttle shook violently.

"We struck something," Axel said.

"An asteroid?" Quinn asked.

"It's an energy field," Axel replied.

"What's our status?" Quinn asked Jeremy.

"The hull is undamaged, but the energy field is keeping us from getting closer. I'm scanning for the source. Once I do, we might be able to fly around it."

Quinn activated the comms channel to Tier 1. "Thanks for the warning," Quinn said to Cameron.

"Don't mention it. I would've warned you sooner, but the shield wasn't active until you passed through the L1 Lagrange point. There must be hidden sensors somewhere. I don't think your shuttle will be able to pick them up. The construct interface is suggesting you return until we find a way around it."

The channel went dead the moment she finished her

message. The shuttle rocked violently. "Pull us away from the planet," Quinn said.

"I already did, but a charged field has surrounded us," Axel replied.

"Any way we can muscle through it?"

Axel entered a few navigation commands on the panel. Wild jarring followed. "Losing partial inertial dampeners. Something's interfering with the hull coating."

Quinn frowned. "That's impossible."

"Not impossible since it's happening. My guess is it has something to do with the envelope surrounding us."

"Cameron, can you jettison a reinforced nano-tether?" Quinn asked.

"I can try, but it's made from the same material as the hull."

Jeremy interrupted. "What is that?"

Quinn squinted. A multicolored fissure on the shuttle interior exploded into a mixture of shimmering bright shades. The hues ranged from a deep indigo to a light, iridescent pink. They blended and swirled together, creating a captivating kaleidoscope of color. Deeper blues and purples formed a base, while the lighter pinks and oranges layered on top, creating a stunning contrast.

The fissure grew larger into a blur of motion. A loud pop rang out from the inside of the shuttle, like metal buckling. Before Quinn had time to react, the force of the explosion sucked all three toward the tear in the hull.

Quinn fought against the suction in a vain attempt to snatch the nano-spray. Just before the vacuum of space sucked him out, he quickly attached the satchel holding a sphere to his side. He tapped it against the other haphazardly during the struggle. A bright light engulfed him, and the whooshing sound ceased. He exhaled. The shuttle stopped rocking. Only he remained mobile.

Quinn wasn't sure how long the pocket of slowed time would last. He lunged toward the nano-spray, assuming the worst, and sprayed a wide coating over the entire fissure. As he did, the bubble around him oscillated. It was as if waves of gravity rolled through him. Time resumed its normal motion.

Jeremy stared at Quinn's position and the nano-gel that now secured the fissure and then turned his gaze toward Quinn, who shrugged. The team took stock of their position and then returned to their panels and analyzed the shuttle's integrity.

"Whatever you did, it's working for now," Axel said. The shuttle plunged hard, and all three smacked into the roof. "We've lost partial inertial . . ." Axel trailed off.

Unsecured items in the shuttle careened wildly in all directions as if shaken in a blender. Quinn struggled to stay conscious. Several more bright lights formed on the inside of the hull, this time in numerous locations. He attempted to locate the satchel strap holding the spheres but failed to do so. The fissures ballooned into a blinding light, and then blackness overtook him.

CHAPTER 8

Tier 1, Earth 2 Orbit/Multiverse 732, arrival loop/ day 2

QUINN'S SIGHT RETURNED. Cameron tapped away at her holo-panel and scanned the readouts. "I think it's working."

The room shook violently. "Partial internal dampeners activating now," Jeremy said.

On the main screen, an area of pitch black shot out from the center of the central node into a region of space directly in front of them. The region grew larger until it encompassed half the sky in front of them. The change was subtle since they were facing away from Earth and in the opposite direction of the Sun.

"Crap," Quinn said.

In a microsecond, all the stars disappeared. Total darkness surrounded them.

"I'm not getting any readings on the space around us, but we are moving," Jeremy said.

A chime sounded from the newly constructed panel that allowed the spheres to interface with Tier 1. Cameron activated several controls on the interface. "The panel shows we're traveling through the network multiverses."

"What's wrong?" Cameron asked. Quinn gave her a look she'd seen many times and instantly shot an eye of recognition. "Or I should say, what went wrong?"

"We descended in the shuttle, but an energy barrier activated when we reached the L1 Lagrange point. We suspected there might be hidden sensors somewhere. We were scanning for them when an energy bubble swallowed us up before we could return. The only signal we picked up early was a faint reading inside the Great Pyramid. But I think we should hold off on any active sensors of the surface in case that contributed to the activation," Quinn said.

Quinn thought for a moment. "I'm going to steal some time," he said and headed toward the simulation room.

Quinn reflected on what Cameron explained earlier regarding Sentry. He could've logged into the streamlined version in the control room but hoped he'd be able to access Sentry with all the bells and whistles so he could brainstorm while in time dilation mode. He just wasn't sure if he could find the relaxed mental state Cameron had. That's when another thought occurred to him.

Quinn doubled back for the control room. On the return trip, the hallway suddenly jostled side to side. He lost his balance and then tapped his cortical implant. "Cameron, what just happened?"

"That energy bubble you mentioned before. Well, it just activated."

Quinn scuttled faster, steadying himself in a vain attempt to move forward. Before he made it, a blinding light exploded and faded into black.

Tier 1, Earth 2 orbit, arrival loop/day 3

Quinn's sight returned. Cameron tapped away at her holo-panel and scanned the readouts. "I think it's working."

While Quinn didn't have time to activate the spheres, he at least knew his mental time-travel ability was working. He wasn't sure how much residual dark matter he had left to loop since his team still hadn't completely discovered a way to measure it, but he had another loop to think about it.

The room shook violently. "Partial internal dampeners activating now," Jeremy said.

On the main screen, an area of pitch black shot out from the center of the central node into a region of space directly in front of them. The region grew larger until it encompassed half the sky in front of them. The change was subtle since they were facing away from Earth and in the opposite direction of the Sun.

"Not again," Quinn said.

In a microsecond, all the stars disappeared. Total darkness surrounded them.

"I'm not getting any readings on the space around us, but we are moving," Jeremy said.

A chime sounded from the newly constructed panel that allowed the spheres to interface with Tier 1. Cameron activated several controls on the interface. "The panel indicates we're traveling through the network multiverses."

"What's wrong?" Cameron asked. Quinn gave her a look she'd seen many times and instantly shot an eye of recognition. "Or I should say, what went wrong?"

"We descended in the shuttle, but an energy barrier

activated when we reached the L1 Lagrange point. We suspected there might be hidden sensors somewhere. We were scanning for them when an energy bubble swallowed us up before we could return. The only signal we picked up early was a faint reading inside the Great Pyramid. That was the first time. The second time, the energy bubble arrived before we even left. I think whoever has that signal on the surface already knows we're here. I'm going to try something else," Quinn said.

Quinn retrieved three of the spheres that powered their journey and tapped them in a specific sequence. A second later, gravity waves shot outward through the entire control room and beyond. He wasn't sure how long the time bubble would last and bolted toward the simulation room.

Once Quinn arrived, he thrust on the visor with his mental commands already running and landed in what could only be described as a *Total Recall* moment, where his mind took him to another world. Immediately he found himself in the sand-strewn desert next to the Great Pyramid.

Sentry, are you there? he thought to himself. Nothing responded.

Any insight into how an energy shield might go undetected or how it might detect us? He waited but still got no response.

Several hundred yards of desert separated him from the Great Pyramid. He glanced at both sides. On the right, a dust trail appeared in the distance, maybe two kilometers.

"Sentry, you there?" he said, this time aloud. There was still no response.

He wasn't sure what might be riding closer in the trail of dust but didn't think it would be anything he wanted to discover, so he jogged forward. Every sense within the simulation was indistinguishable from reality, at least as far as he could tell. He tasted and breathed in the dryness of the air, the warmth of the sun on his skin, and the pounding heart in his chest as the dust trail inched closer.

He halved the distance between himself and the pyramid, still only seeing himself and the growing dust trail. He wondered if anyone might be around the other sides. He kept running and hoped he could find enough time out of sight from whatever was approaching to calm his thoughts and connect with Sentry.

Figures emerged within the small cloud of dust. He made out only one initially, then two, and then three. One figure was riding on something he couldn't quite make out, a horse or camel, he wasn't sure. He didn't think camels moved that fast, so he assumed it was a horse of some kind.

Quinn hurried to the side of the pyramid and moved as far out of sight as he could while looking for anything to give him cover and keep whoever was approaching from seeing him.

"Let's try this again," he said aloud. He closed his eyes and reflected on what Cameron had said regarding slowing her breathing before Sentry appeared for the first time in the simulation. He slowed his breath and followed a simple mindfulness practice. *Sentry, are you there?* he thought.

He waited, calming his breath, striving to clear his mind of the looming, albeit unreal, danger. His main concern was to relax enough to either activate Sentry or access his mind, the mechanics of which remained somewhat mysterious.

Ah, Quinn. Yes, I'm here, the voice in Quinn's mind replied.

The desert setting bled into white and then receded into a completely new location. The pyramids vanished, and in their place towered the White Cliffs of Dover. Waves pounded on the shore far below. The sun hung low and bathed the expansive English Channel in golden light. The majestic cliffs rose from the shoreline, and their gleaming white faces reflected the sun's rays.

The cliffs towered over the water like a Medieval fortress wall. Salt and seaweed mingled with the sweet fragrance of wildflowers growing in the grassy meadows up to the edge. The rolling waves crashed against the base, echoing in a constant background noise.

A second later, a promenade with several opulent benches materialized a few feet from the precipice. Its tiles glistened to a high sheen, reflecting the sun. Intricate patterns decked the tiles. Benches and flowerpots lined the walkway. Their bright colors contrasted against the muted narrow pavement surrounding it.

A figure appeared, sitting on the bench closest to Quinn, and beckoned him to sit.

"Care for some tea?" Sentry asked.

Quinn sat and gazed upon the setting, facing the English Channel. "How much of what's happening outside do you know?"

Sentry brought the teacup to his lips. "Most people prefer Earl Gray or English Breakfast, but I fell in love with Yorkshire long ago."

Despite the urgency, Quinn embraced the calm and allowed the setting to get him out of his head. "Maybe I will take a cup."

A porcelain teacup resting on a small plate appeared on the table in front of him. Vapors rose from the liquid and quickly disappeared. Quinn brought the tea to his lips and inhaled its earthy notes before he sipped.

"I only know what's happening to the construct and what's holding it. From what I can sense, there's an energy barrier from the Old Ones, who you know as The Way. I recognize its frequency. Beyond that, I know nothing," Sentry said.

"The energy bubble, or whatever it is, already killed me twice. It's in the process of doing it again. I've activated the spheres and created a pocket of delayed time. They collapsed the bubble when I was returning from the shuttle. How is that even possible?" Quinn asked.

"It's good you came here and accessed the reverse time dilation, but from what I'm reading, you're racing against the clock. You will die again once you leave the simulation."

"So much for coming here then."

Sentry sipped quietly as if pondering Quinn's statement. "You shouldn't be too surprised. You've embarked on a perilous path, as have your companions. And despite your likely death, all is not lost."

"What can you tell me exactly about the Old Ones and how they are interfering with the time bubble?"

"My memory banks give me a few specific details on setting up beacons around a fixed radius. With three, they can create a sphere of influence. Any use of the time travel technology they've developed can be dampened, though not completely suppressed within that radius of influence. Based on the information you provided, any use of the time bubble won't last more than a minute at most. That won't, however, stop you from using other types of time travel or any technology that operates on a frequency different than the spheres."

"How can you be so certain I'm going to die when I leave here?"

"That's the other thing. The spheres you took from the planet where you found my construct were once controlled by the Old Ones. While you are within their controlling radius, the spheres will act as a beacon."

Quinn wondered if he could eventually reverse-engineer the spheres.

"Can they detect the spheres once we return home?"

"Only if they can create a new region of influence. So provided that doesn't happen, they won't be able to. But anywhere you travel where they do, the spheres will give away your location and allow them to piggyback on the signal and turn the signal itself into a weapon to destroy you."

"Is there anything you can do to hide our use of them?"

Sentry's eyes gazed deeper as if pondering Quinn's question. He sipped more tea and inhaled, then turned toward the cliffs. "The short answer is I don't know. The way the technology works impacts everything around it in the current universe. On the surface, it would appear impossible. But your Arthur C. Clark once said, 'The only way of discovering the limits of the possible is to venture a little way past them into the impossible.'"

"How much time do I have here? How much can you help me?"

"Less than you need, a few days at most, maybe, in what would feel like your linear time. Certainly, not enough to find a way to shield the use of the sphere from triangulation."

"What if we don't have to hide their activation, just the spheres themselves? You said they're only detected if we are within the sensor region. We can just move outside that area."

"Yes, but then you wouldn't be able to use them."

"True, but we may not need to. We only need to avoid detection," Quinn said.

"The only problem is that you've already used them for your arrival. The address you've plotted has you arriving within that zone."

Quinn thought for a moment. He wondered why they encountered trouble only after crossing the L1 Lagrange point during their first entry. In later instances, the spheres revealed their position immediately upon arrival.

"Why didn't the energy field appear when we first appeared?"

"The only possible answer is that you did something different that changed the outcome. You are the only variable. When you died and your mental time travel brought you to the same location in six-dimensional space, you did something or created a change that alerted them to your presence. The L1 Lagrange point is one of the beacon points. My guess is that a second is in the Great Pyramid. A third is someplace else, likely within the solar system."

"What should I do with the time I have left?"

"Discover what you did differently. Start with the moment when things changed, and work backward."

Over the next few days in simulated time, Quinn scrutinized every minor deviation until time ran out.

CHAPTER 9

Tier 1, Earth 2 orbit/Multiverse 732, the descent, loop 14

CAMERON TAPPED AWAY at her holo-panel and scanned the readouts. "I think it's working."

The room shook violently. "Partial internal dampeners activating now," Jeremy said.

On the main screen, an area of pitch black shot out from the center of the central node into a region of space directly in front of them. The region grew larger until it encompassed half the sky in front of them. The change was subtle since they were facing away from Earth and in the opposite direction from the Sun.

"A wormhole is opening up directly in front of us," Quinn said.

In a microsecond, all the stars disappeared. Total darkness surrounded them.

"I'm not getting any readings on the surrounding space, but we are moving," Jeremy added.

A chime sounded from the newly constructed panel that

interfaced with the spheres. Cameron activated several of its controls. "The panel shows we're traveling through the network multiverses."

"How much longer will it take?" Quinn asked, careful to word his conversations exactly as he'd done before.

"That question is a bit complicated to answer, but from the readings, we should be there in what will feel like a few seconds," Cameron replied.

"And I'm assuming it should be instantaneous relative to our Earth and time of departure."

"That should be the case, but we'll have to wait until we return to confirm that."

A small area of stars emerged on the screen, spreading rapidly until the blackness vanished.

"We're here," Jeremy said.

"Pull up Earth on the viewscreen and see if we can get an image of the surface," Quinn said.

"Done," Jeremy replied. Every continent rested in its correct location. Nothing out of the ordinary stood out from the distant view.

"Are we picking up any artificial satellites or communications from the planet?" Quinn asked.

"Checking now," Cameron said. Her face remained stoic as she scanned through the readings.

"No satellites are in orbit that I can detect, or anywhere in the solar system, for that matter. No communications channels of any kind on the planet except for one single location."

"Let me guess," Quinn said.

"Zooming in for a closer look," Jeremy said.

The view screen displayed a wide angle of the Great Pyramid at the center. All other pyramids appeared there as well, with much less wear than Quinn remembered them having.

"Are we in the right time and place?"

Cameron entered a few commands. "If these readings are accurate, yes. The images of the surface and the current state of infrastructure support that as well."

"What can you tell me about the reading you're getting from within the Great Pyramid?"

"Not much. It's partially masked by the structure itself, but I don't see any direct attempt to hide its signature. It matches the frequency we identified from analyzing the video. That's about all I can detect. It's very faint," Cameron said.

Quinn entered some queries into the streamlined interface, the same ones he entered before the time loop. Quinn took the same crew as last time. This loop, however, he would leave the spheres behind.

One hour later, Quinn loaded into one of the small shuttles attached to Tier 1. Quinn kept the portable med station and food printer along with rations but alerted the group to a few changes before they boarded. The pilot, Axel, was a seasoned pro and took Quinn's updates in stride. Quinn also informed them there would be additional commands once they boarded the shuttle.

"We're going to avoid any scans of the surface. I'm going to give you the coordinates. What I didn't tell you before was that we're currently in a time loop. At least I am. I'll go to the point where we entered the singularity within this multiverse. That's as far as I can go when I'm not in ours."

"Tell us what we need to know, Boss," Axel said.

"They know we're here. Unfortunately, there's nothing

we can do about that. We rode it here, and it's our way back. The spheres will activate an energy bubble that will collapse the shuttle if we bring them along, so I left them."

"So this is a one-way mission?" Axel asked.

"Quite possibly for you, yes. And if I run out of the dark matter that powers my mental time travel, it might be for me as well. I don't know how many more trips around the wheel I have left. I'm still working on figuring that part out. This is the first time we made it to the shuttle since our first try, and I think leaving the spheres will keep us alive until we return unless something else on the surface kills us."

"How many times?" Jeremy asked.

"This time makes fourteen, but it's only the second time we've been on the shuttle. The first, an energy field activated once we reached the L1 Lagrange point. I activated the spheres to create a time bubble, but it collapsed. That was the end of it. The spheres act as a beacon. We should be able to land on the surface since we don't have them. We'll just need to do it right the first time."

"I've got your back. I just wish we had more intel on whoever's doing this. Maybe we could find a way to get in their head," Axel said.

That would be the Old Ones, as Sentry called them, but Quinn knew it was possible The Way had other groups duped and doing their dirty work for them without even knowing about it, which would make navigating the surface once they arrived all the more difficult.

"I like the way you think. If you come up with some ideas, let me know."

"Will do, Boss."

"Passing the Lagrange point now," Jeremy said.

Quinn reinforced several areas of the hull interior with nanospray before their departure and took a few other precautions in case the energy barrier appeared.

"I'm not picking up any energy variances. The shuttle might be undetected," Jeremy added.

"The spheres may not be their only means of detection, but I'll take it for now. Continue the same descent pattern, and let's see how far we can get down. And I think we need another change," Quinn said, glancing at Axel.

"What do you need, Boss?"

"I want you to come down to the surface with us. We'll need to conceal the shuttle, but I no longer think it's riskier to keep it on the surface than in the air. I think it's more likely you'll be discovered orbiting the planet than stationary below. And I know we can use all the hands we can get once we get down there."

"Fine by me. I've been itching to vent my frustration. Looks like now I might finally get the chance."

Axel clenched his fist, anticipating the first tangible foe to confront since kidnappers took his teenage sister before the supernova. No one ever found her or what happened to her. All they had was a grainy video of a couple of thugs coming up from behind and tossing her into an old Chevy at a local mini-mart.

He spent months searching. It took all his restraint to keep from bashing in the skulls of any young punk that slightly fit the description. The leads never panned out, but whenever he found any of them were up to no good, that didn't stop him from getting in a few good licks, just enough to teach them a lesson and keep himself out of jail.

After the months receded into years, he put his frustration

into his work. His old military unit got recalled to work on the government project that eventually went belly up. That's when he threw his hat in with Quinn's array company, and the rest is history.

Many array crew members shared unique yet similar pasts and a temperament suited for the solitude of space. The vastness of the cosmos offered ample opportunity for introspection, a prospect that often unsettled most people.

The shuttle continued its descent with comms off just in case they were being monitored, which Quinn suspected The Way would do if they were able.

"We should land the ship down three clicks away from the Great Pyramid. Hopefully, that will keep us from being detected at the entrance while still being close enough to head there on foot."

"And close enough for a quick exit," Axel suggested.

"Exactly. But we're going to have to land blind, visuals only. We're probably safe, but I don't want to take any chances," Quinn said.

The designers equipped the shuttle with four small windows exactly for the current scenario. Quinn already had opened two upon their departure. Safety protocols forced him to wait until they were ten thousand feet above the surface before opening the next two.

"So what's the plan when we get to the surface?" Jeremy asked.

"Still working that part out, but not for lack of trying. I just don't know the situation on the surface yet. I'm hoping we can find a way into the pyramid undetected and search until we find either our alt selves or the signal. But I don't think that's likely without running into some resistance. If the locals aren't carrying anything acquired from The Way, we should be able to handle them with little effort and without hurting them much."

"That's a big if," Jeremy said.

"We've got weapons. I just don't want to have to kill anyone if I don't have to, especially if they're innocent."

"I wouldn't get too bent out of shape about doing what you need to survive. But we'll follow your lead, Boss," Axel said.

Quinn opened the two additional windows. Light beamed in from the two newly opened portholes. Jeremy was closest to their position and snuck a peak. "This side is clear."

Axel viewed the other side. "This side too."

"Let's move," Quinn said.

CHAPTER 10

EARTH 2/MULTIVERSE 732, PLANET SURFACE, LOOP 14, JUST AFTER LANDING

QUINN AND CREW hurried from the shuttle, gear in tow, and flashed a reflective mirror to hopefully alert Cameron to their safe arrival. They'd relied on old-school methods after deciding to stay comms silent.

The crew scuttled back from the shuttle far enough away to let Axel activate the cloaking device, which just meant burrowing the shuttle underground. It wouldn't work in urban environments where slabs of metal and concrete often got in the way, but the special properties attached to the shuttle hull, similar to those on the array, allowed the shuttle to sink below the surface.

In less than thirty seconds, the shuttle concealed itself. All Quinn needed to do was push the activation button, and the shuttle would rise above the surface in the same amount of time. They'd also be able to fly the shuttle remotely with a similar activation sequence. He wasn't sure if the shuttle would activate the energy field from the prior loops, but so far, it'd only occurred with the orbs present.

Once they recorded their position, in case they returned on foot, they marched off toward the Great Pyramid. "I'll watch our six, Boss," Axel said.

The memory of their alternate group being hunted down by unseen pursuers unnerved Quinn. He reflected on the laser weapons and more than several combatants moving quickly toward the team. They could already be gone from the area, but he didn't want to make any assumptions.

Normally at this point, Quinn would activate his cortical implant and scan the area, but he didn't want to use it just yet. He'd also instructed the rest of the party to avoid using them until he gave the go-ahead, just in case The Way had a way to track them or the implants contributed to the activation of the energy shield.

Axel brought a small pair of sand-colored binoculars to his eyes. Most of their gear was the same color, in hopes they would camouflage themselves enough in the desert to avoid any unwanted scrutiny.

"I see something," Axel said.

He handed the binoculars to Quinn, who spied through them. "Looks like a click and a half left of where we need to go. It might be far enough away to avoid them, but we should take the right flank just in case."

The crew each sipped water and then slogged toward the Great Pyramid at double speed.

Half a click into their slog, Axel alerted the group to something approaching. "They're moving quickly, Boss. What do you want to do?"

"Ready the weapons, but keep up the pace. Whoever

they are, they can catch up to us," Quinn said. There was nowhere to hide anyway, so he thought they might as well keep moving toward where they needed to go until they were certain they were in danger.

Jeremy stole a glance through the binoculars and squinted. "They look like a group of people, locals maybe. I count at least six," he said.

They increased their pace, and so did the group following them. "I see at least two women and a kid," he added a short while later.

Quinn's chest relaxed. He was about to continue his stride unabated and then stopped. "We're going to rest here until they reach us."

"Boss?"

"This may be our chance to get some intel. If they turn out to be hostiles, we'll deal with them, but the women and children don't suggest they'd be that much of a threat or at least any more of a threat than who was on the video. It's worth the risk. Let's put up the tarp and take a few minutes of rest."

Dr. Green didn't hesitate to pull equipment out of the bag he'd been lugging around, and Jeremy quickly assisted. Once they had the small canopy in place to shield out the sun, the crew downed some water and half a ration bar each as they waited for the arriving group.

Jeremy held the binoculars to his eyes, unflinching as the people drew closer. Axel glared at Jeremy, who continued to hog the binocs without saying a word. "See anything interesting?"

Jeremy chewed his ration bar, still glaring. Axel relented and shifted his focus to slowly growing fuzzy dots. "I count eight, maybe nine. Three women, two children, and at least three adult males."

Quinn strained his focus and then held out his hand for the binocs from Jeremy, who still had them glued to his sockets. "Now you've got me curious," Quinn said.

Jeremy handed them off to Quinn, who peered through. "Ah. Now I get it."

Dr. Green and Axel raised their brows. Quinn passed the binocs off to Axel. Jeremy only gave Axel a second before he yanked them back and returned to his entranced state. "She's a beauty. Can't say I blame you."

Jeremy gazed at the group through the specs. A young woman stood on the side, mid-twenties he guessed. Bland sand-colored scarves hid some but not all of her flawless copper skin.

"Better ask her out while you've got the chance," Axel said.

Jeremy said nothing. Dr. Green was about to add something, but Quinn gave him a look that made him back off. He didn't want Jeremy's already foul mood to stew. Better to let him distract himself.

The group stopped for a moment off in the distance before resuming. Quinn assumed they must've finally noticed them and were likely deciding on whether to continue.

"I don't see any weapons," Jeremy said.

"You're clearly focused on other things," Axel replied. "But don't worry. I promise I won't say a word."

Jeremy inhaled, and Quinn sensed Jeremy was exercising more restraint than he let on. Quinn stole the lenses a moment before returning them. "I think you're right, but let's remain ready just in case."

Both Axel and Jeremy remained glued to the group who strode closer, each focusing their attention on the woman. When the group of nomads were in striking distance, Quinn rushed ahead to greet them, unsure if they would even understand him.

Quinn waved to them. "My name is Quinn, and these are my friends. We traveled a long way to get here, and we're looking for another group of people who look like us."

Quinn made out nine figures. Three women, two children, and four men. Two of the women each had one child by their side, and by their worn skin and tired eyes, he assumed they were in their later thirties. The men, he couldn't tell, but there was a range between thirty and fifty. Both kids stood less than four feet tall among the much taller adults.

A middle-aged man, whom Quinn assumed was their leader, stepped forward. When he did, the young woman Jeremy and Axel had been ogling from a distance became visible. He understood why Jeremy was so fixated on her. He averted his eyes and returned his attention to the man now only a few feet in front of him.

"I have seen your people," the leader said.

"You speak English," Dr. Green added.

"I know many languages, and I've seen those who you seek. Come. I'll take you to a safe place," he continued. Axel eyed the men suspiciously, but Quinn signaled to follow the man's lead.

Jeremy fixed his gaze on the young woman only to turn away occasionally in a vain attempt not to appear as if he was staring. Judging by the looks of everyone else around them, he wasn't doing a great job at it, but the young woman appeared unfazed and difficult to read.

They uprooted their gear and followed the group half a click northeast before they stopped at a flat spot in the desert, still hundreds of yards from any visible landmark and a little less than half a kilometer between either the Great Pyramid and the shuttle Quinn and crew had buried. Axel squinted and scanned the periphery in confusion.

"Down here. Follow me, and be quick," the leader said, lifting a hatch that was concealed by a tan rug.

Quinn heeded his words, and the rest followed closely behind, down a series of short stairwells that led to a large underground bunker.

"My name is Ubuntu, and this is my daughter, Kira," he said, motioning toward the beautiful woman who still held Jeremy's gaze.

"You know why we're here?" Quinn asked.

"I'm hoping it's the same reason the others came."

"Which is?" Axel asked.

"To stop our common enemy," he paused and then added, "if that is your aim."

"And what can you tell us of this enemy?" Quinn said.

The young woman stepped forward toward her father. "They are terrible. They've taken everything we had, and they still want more."

"What do they want?" Dr. Green added.

"They want to end worlds. As to why, I cannot say. All I know is that they're using this world—" he paused "—our world, in an attempt to destroy others."

"The beacon," Axel said.

"Yes. I believe that is what you speak of, but it's dangerous."

The moment Ubuntu spoke those words, the faces in his group dropped. He continued, "Our world changed. Pieces of our world vanished until there was almost nothing left. Our world was once like yours, but this beacon has brought back our past, one long forgotten."

"What do you mean?" Dr. Green asked.

"I know your language because this Earth was very similar to what I'm assuming is the Earth from which you came, as well as those who came before you, the ones you must be looking for."

Quinn stopped him. "Was there a supernova in your world?"

"That is when it all started. Someone quite like yourself became a savior to our world and built a large object in the sky. It saved us from the explosion, but then—" he paused.

"Parts of our world disappeared," Kira cut in.

They stood silent for a moment before Quinn spoke. "That fits with what we know. They destroy worlds and return them to the Stone Age if possible. Usually, they don't do it so quickly, but I guess every world is different. I only know bits and pieces. We came here because we followed a group who sent us a distress call. I think they may have been looking for the beacon. This world could be the center of their big plan or at least part of it. Do you know how we can get inside?" Quinn asked.

"We can show you the path, but it's heavily guarded," Kira added.

Quinn motioned for them to continue, and then slowly advanced down a torchlit corridor. As they moved ahead, the tunnels expanded in all directions. Several hundred yards down the pathway, they emerged into a large maze-like complex that was more brightly lit and bustling with activity.

"This is some kind of underground village," Dr. Green said.

"What exactly happened?" Quinn asked.

"Section by section, they transformed large tracts of land. Not just the land, but everything above and below. They stole what was here and traded places with what was on another Earth. Piece by piece they stole our world, the best of it, and replaced it with theirs," Kira said.

"Did they do that over the whole planet or just here?" Quinn asked.

"They did it everywhere. They started with mines and water and then moved whole cities."

"Why would they do that?" Jeremy asked.

"Their universe is dying. And there are different versions of them from different universes, some in different stages of decline. From what we've gathered, they've been mapping out a network of Earths and other worlds across this multiverse and others that they can plunder. We had spies in their camps once before, but now they are all gone."

She paused before Ubuntu added, "Killed."

Quinn reflected on the implications. The web The Way wove in his head was simply too vast to comprehend. There must be countless iterations of the organization, and they all might be doing things uniquely. He wondered if they coordinated with the different versions or if it was just some chaotic mess that played out across the vast expanse, a free-for-all between whoever had access to the same technology. There would be limitless universes to plunder but also infinite worlds on the brink of death.

"Do you think there's anything you can do to stop them?" Quinn asked.

Ubuntu's face changed. "I honestly don't know, but their power comes from within the Great Pyramid. It's the most dangerous and safest place to be. That's why we've built this here. We can take you to the edge of our new home, but from there, you will be on your own."

Quinn wondered what kind of safeguards were in place around the beacon and only wished he could risk scanning the area more thoroughly. "I think there's only one way we'll find what we need. We have to go there," Quinn said.

CHAPTER 11

EARTH 2/MULTIVERSE 732, BENEATH THE GREAT PYRAMID, LOOP 14

JEREMY TROTTED CLOSELY beside Kira, doing his best to make small talk as she led the way forward toward the Great Pyramid. "You have a lot of interesting stories, and I hope you find what you're looking for, for all our sakes. But I have to leave now and stay with my people," she said.

"I hope this isn't the last time we see you," Jeremy said.

She smiled, but a haunting glint appeared in her eyes. "We've lost many friends who've tried to stop them, so for your sake, I hope you're right."

Jeremy stayed glued to Kira's face until Ubuntu spoke, "You'll need to follow this path a hundred yards until you come to a small bend. Follow it all the way left until you reach a false dead end. You'll need to push until it opens. Once it closes, you won't be able to return this way. You'll be on your own," he said.

With that, Quinn and his group took their leave in the direction of the Great Pyramid. Jeremy waved to Kira. She smiled again but didn't return the gesture.

"I feel for you, man. I do," Axel said.

"Quit playing with me," Jeremy replied.

"I'm not messin' with you, man. She might've been interested."

"What makes you think we won't see her again?"

"You're right. Maybe we will. There's hope for you yet," Axel replied.

Quinn ignored the banter and led the way forward. The corridor grew narrow and dark. Once they arrived at the bend, the temperature dropped ten degrees, and an eerie sound emerged.

The air buzzed as scarab beetles flooded from the passage. Their mass movement drummed loudly in their ears. Clicks and hums blended seamlessly into a continuous hiss that enveloped the surroundings.

"Let's get the hell out of here," Dr. Green said.

"Don't worry. I've got your back," Axel said.

The swarm rushed toward them. Axel lifted his leg and stomped.

"Don't," Quinn said.

Axel stood on one leg as the swarm rushed by, leaving them alone.

"They're harmless. But I'm pretty sure it's a sign we're getting close. My guess is we're getting closer to the beacon. It may emit a frequency that's scaring them," Quinn added.

"I think you're correct," Dr. Green said.

The swarm receded and the walkway grew quiet once more. Quinn scanned the nearby area and strode a few paces. The pathway ended a few more steps ahead, and the last few beams of light emitted from the closest lantern faded to pitch.

Quinn touched the cold, solid wall. "I think it's here.

Let's push together." They placed their hands on the center of the wall. "Now push," he said.

The stone wall slid forward with a harsh scrape and moved unexpectedly long before revealing a space where two side walls then converged. Quinn sauntered in, and the others followed suit. Every few meters, the forward wall retracted and the side walls closed in. The process quickened as they delved deeper and forced them to sprint at the end.

Just as they approached their limits, the transformation stopped, and they found themselves in another larger corridor. Faint specs of light filtered in from above in a linear path. Dr. Green attempted to get close enough to one of the light beams to peer outside. "Somebody give me a lift."

Axel interlocked his fingers and placed his palms facing up. Dr. Green used them for a step and thrust himself up, getting as close to the small crevice as possible. He steadied himself against the wall. "I can see open ground on the left. We're underneath the base of the left-corner entrance to the pyramid. It should extend 230 meters forward and to the right. So I think we should move down the right side of this corridor and then take the first left when we find one," Dr. Green said.

Quinn turned behind him. They were sealed off from where they had come. The only direction they could move was left or right. "Right it is then."

On Tier 1, Cameron returned to the simulator. She activated the visor and almost immediately controlled her breathing to slow her heart rate and create the desired brainwaves needed to enter reverse mental time dilation.

"Welcome back. I'm assuming you want to help Quinn on the ground," Sentry said.

"I want to discover what's causing the energy field and see if we can disable it or shield ourselves so we can communicate with the surface. Heck, I'll settle for a basic scan. We're still not exactly clear on how or when it gets activated. I know using the spheres activates it. But there's more to it than that."

Sentry changed the environment settings and brought her to the same French chateau she found herself in when she first fully accessed the program. She exhaled.

"Yes, I do sense you like this place. I'm fond of it myself."

Cameron sat for a moment and inhaled the fresh scents around her, the strings of flowers, the slight aroma of fresh honey and milk in the small kitchen.

"Have you told us everything you know about the spheres and how they work?"

"I have on a conscious level, but I may be missing some less obvious subtleties with this form. We can run a simulated environment and see if the construct might reveal something my conscious mind has missed. My biggest benefit is that I can tell you directly, but only if I can see it on the conscious level. Sometimes to synthesize knowledge and see all the possibilities, you have to look beyond the conscious."

"In that case, put me back in the simulation."

"As you wish."

Near the underground edge of the Great Pyramid, Quinn's group traveled a hundred meters right, and then the corridor grew shrouded in darkness. "Quiet," Dr. Green said.

The chatter and footsteps halted. All that remained was

the whispering wind, like a faint whistle. "You hear that? We must be close. The passage to the way in should be on the left side of this wall."

Jeremy shifted left and cupped a hand behind his ear, stepping forward. The whispers increased to a howl. Suddenly, the wind ceased and gave way to the faint click of pincers cutting through the darkness. The rhythmic scuttling of tiny exoskeletons echoed with each calculated step. Minute vibrations reached Jeremy's right foot. He tilted his head down, and the swarm engulfed his shoe. "Scorpions!" he shouted. He danced in a janky motion, shaking right and then left.

Axel aimed his light toward Jeremy's feet, where a swarm of around ten Egyptian fat-tailed scorpions, each around three inches long, made their way up the neck of Jeremy's shoe. Axel elongated a baton and swiped at the two with pincers retracted and ready to strike.

Jeremy jumped up as high as he could and huffed, coming down on two or three at a time with a crunch. "Those *will* kill you," Dr. Green said. Jeremy kept hopping a while before Dr. Green added, "And unfortunately, we don't have any anti-venom."

"Not helpful," Jeremy said, still dancing the janky dance.

Axel and Quinn stomped on the remaining scorpions that scuttled nearby. Axel kept swinging the baton at the few that found their way up Jeremy's shoe.

"Why is it just me? Why aren't they crawling up your legs?"

"Must be your animal magnetism," Axel said.

Jeremy said nothing but continued to hop a while longer until the swarm stopped and all visible scorpions ceased all but the slightest motion from a few stingers near-death.

After the dust settled, Dr. Green turned left to face the open corridor that lay in front of them. There, in the flickering torchlight, a baroque golden sarcophagus appeared. Its surface mirrored the reflected light in a dance of fiery patterns.

"Hooooly . . . crap," Dr. Green said.

The crypt stood tall and regal, adorned with intricate engravings that told ancient tales of gods and pharaohs.

As they drew closer, the surface painted fleeting patterns upon the walls. Jeremy stretched his hand forward just over the brim. "Don't touch it. It could be booby-trapped," Dr. Green said.

"Yeah. You don't want any more of those scorpions swarming all over you."

"That wasn't my fault," Jeremy said.

"You sure about that?" Axel asked.

"I doubt what we're looking for is in this room. This must be bait," Quinn said.

"Can't fault your reasoning there, Boss," Axel said.

For a few moments, they stood motionless. Quinn analyzed his options, and then an odd color of the room became apparent. "Are you guys seeing what I'm seeing?"

The crew stood staring at the center of the bejeweled sarcophagus, inspecting it closer. "You're going to have to be a little more specific," Jeremy said.

"The shade of the room keeps changing. It's a shuttle shift, almost as if . . ." Quinn stopped himself.

"Something is flashing," Dr. Green finished.

"Yes. Something is flashing."

Axel and Jeremy shook their gaze from the center of the

room and eyed the walls, hunting for the slightest change in tone. "I see it, too, Boss."

"Yeah. I see it. It's like a slight red or orange, and then it disappears for a second," Jeremy added.

Axel dropped to the floor, scouring the ground. Dr. Green inspected the corners and around the sarcophagus. Jeremy and Quinn eyed the walls. The process continued for several minutes. Jeremy lightly punched a wall with his closed fist. "Where the hell is that thing?"

No one replied, but Quinn roamed around the same section. "I think I see a subtle difference in intensity on that wall, which means it should be coming from over here," he said from the opposite side of the room.

Axel met his gaze but from the floor. He felt with his hands until he hit the corner perpendicular to where Quinn kept his focus. "Under here. There's a gap."

Everyone dropped to the ground.

"I think I . . ." Steps marching toward them interrupted him. Quinn shot up and twisted in the direction of the approaching feet.

Four strangely clad men strode into the room. Their attire was a fusion of sleek metallic fabrics and flowing, iridescent robes, shimmering and shifting with every movement.

Goosebumps rose on Quinn's arms. The men's piercing eyes swept across the assembled group. Quinn felt as if he'd just fallen into an episode of *Stargate SG-1*. One of the men spoke. He couldn't understand him, and then he realized the language was something completely foreign.

Dr. Green squinted. Quinn assumed he was attempting to recognize the language patterns without success.

The men charged forward right up to Quinn's face. "Come with us now," the man closest said.

"I guess they know English after all," Axel said.

That remark earned him a knock against the back of his head.

"Ay, what the hell, man?"

Quinn gave Axel a look that told him not to do anything just yet. He signaled them to follow, and they turned. Dr. Green stayed behind a few feet and took his time. All the men wore sheathed swords, which clashed with the robes that Quinn suspected were coated with exotic material. One of the men tapped a square object on his side. The walls beside them lurched away and revealed a well-lit large chamber.

Jeremy gasped. He first saw her exposed bronze leg and the ropes tied around her ankle. Kira lay bound on the floor with a man standing over her. She writhed from left to right, attempting to wiggle free from the thick rope that bound her waist and wrists. A gag in her mouth quelled her speech to muted, intelligible notes.

The leader of the guard group motioned for them to sit down. When they hesitated, his hand went for the butt of his sword. "We get the message," Dr. Green said and sat down first. Jeremy went next. Axel grumbled but sat down next to Quinn.

Once seated, the men tied up each of Quinn's group. Quinn sat on the hard ground as they grabbed his arms, placed them behind his back, and wrapped a thick twine tightly around his wrists. Once secure, they secured each member.

The twine chafed Quinn's wrists with barely any movement, like rough burlap. He wasn't sure if that was just what they used to tie up prisoners in that situation or if they were just doing it to add a little more discomfort. The longer he sat, the harder he found it to maintain a position without irritating his skin.

The men left Quinn's group squirming. After a few minutes, Quinn wondered how long they would need to sit there before someone returned. "At least they didn't gag us," Axel said. "You know," Axel continued, his voice carrying a playful tone, "if I had known we were going to a bonding retreat, I would have brought some marshmallows and graham crackers. We could've turned this into a proper campfire gathering."

"But they did gag *her*," Jeremy said, nodding to Kira. "Are you okay, Kira?" he asked.

Kira continued to struggle. She mumbled something, but the gag prevented her from saying anything they could recognize.

Jeremy gritted his teeth. "I want to punch them," he said, stopping as if he were about to say something more.

"Easy there, tiger. I'm pretty sure we'd get clobbered without some extra manpower. We need to use our brains on this one," Axel said.

"They must have her people too unless they've done something worse," Jeremy said.

Kira squirmed, mumbling. Jeremy clenched his fists, his nails digging into his palms. The next few moments stretched out for everyone. Eventually, Kira relaxed as best they assumed she could, and Jeremy relented his rants.

Dr. Green's eyes strained and forehead wrinkled, which Quinn assumed as deep thought. Jeremy remained hypnotized by Kira's plight, and any escape attempt currently eluded Quinn.

"Hey, guys," Dr. Green whispered. Once he had their attention, he wiggled free a small object he'd tucked between his waistband and hip. "I found this underneath the wall just as we were being captured. We might be able to use it to get out of here."

Quinn leaned in to get a better look at the small metallic device that featured a series of buttons and a tiny display screen. His eyebrows furrowed as he studied the mysterious object.

"What is it?" he asked.

Dr. Green's eyes gleamed. "I'm not entirely sure, but it appears to be a high-tech keycard or hacking device. It must have been dropped or hidden here by someone who came before us. It might even be connected to the beacon we've been searching for, or maybe . . ."

The march of steps interrupted him and grew louder. Silence fell over Quinn and his companions. Dr. Green's eyes met Quinn's. With a swift motion, Dr. Green returned the mysterious object to his waistband, concealing it once again. The footsteps drew closer, and the group braced themselves for the arrival of their captors.

The door swung open, and a burly figure stepped inside. He was followed by two more armed men with hardened expressions. They surveyed the room, their eyes lingering on Quinn and his companions before settling on Kira. "Stand up," the burly man commanded.

One of the armed men approached Kira, removing the gag with a swift, almost careless motion. Kira coughed and took a deep breath, and her eyes darted around the room. "Where is it?" the burly man demanded. "Don't bother pretending you don't know what I'm talking about. We've been watching you."

Dr. Green's voice broke the tension. "We don't know what you're talking about. We're innocent civilians caught up in something we don't understand."

The burly man signaled to the others. They rushed forward, shoved Dr. Green in the gut, and then tied a cloth gag in his mouth. "That'll teach you to talk, old man. If we want you to speak, we'll tell you. Otherwise, keep your mouths shut, or we'll do the same to the rest of you."

Once the gag was firmly in place, he shoved Dr. Green again for good measure and then yanked Kira by her hair and dragged her out to the walkway. Once they faded into the shadows, everyone shifted their focus to Jeremy.

"We got your back," Axel said.

Jeremy didn't respond, but from his expression, Quinn assumed Jeremy would take his revenge once they had the opportunity.

Quinn let a few more minutes pass and then signaled for Dr. Green to retrieve the device. "See if you can pass it to Axel."

From their position, Axel was the closest and stood a good chance to shift himself into a position to grab it. "See if you can break free," Quinn said to Axel.

"Already ahead of you there." Axel snapped the bindings in two. "Never get captured without a razor stashed in your back pocket," he added. He made quick work of the bindings on his legs and then freed the rest of them.

Quinn analyzed the device, but before he could process it, a loud explosion rocked the building, shaking its very foundations. The walls trembled, and dust and debris fell from the ceiling. They stumbled, but soon steadied themselves.

Quinn's heart pounded. "This is it. Let's get the hell out of here."

With those words, Quinn, Dr. Green, Jeremy, and Axel sprang into action. They maneuvered through the disarray, using the commotion as cover. Together, they hurried toward the nearest exit and burst through the door and into the nearby empty chamber.

"Keep moving," Quinn said.

They ran down a long, narrow corridor and came to a fork. Quinn headed left, not sure where it led but not wanting to dally longer than he needed to. The corridor extended fifty yards and then split three ways.

"Let's take the center, but we'll mark it on the corner in case we need to retrace it," Quinn said.

They ran twenty yards, and then the shaking resumed. "Another blast," Axel said.

Quinn speculated on what might be causing it. He wasn't sure if it was related to Kira, or if the other version of Quinn's team was involved. It might also have something to do with the device Dr. Green had taken. A fist-sized brick fell squarely on Quinn's head and interrupted his train of thought. "Dammit!" He rubbed his crown. "Keep moving!"

Quinn quickened his pace. The falling stones continued, but the shaking subsided gradually as they pressed on. They arrived at a larger open space. By that point, the shaking had stopped. A brisk wind blew from somewhere and extinguished the one remaining lantern that had lit the space. Dr. Green fumbled for a light but remembered their captors had confiscated their gear. "Axel, you don't happen to have a flashlight hidden somewhere by any chance?"

A tiny light emerged, squelching the darkness. "Behold, the Signature Lite Swiss Army Knife by Victorinox. I take it with me wherever I go," Axel said.

"Where were you hiding that?" Jeremy asked.

"Don't ever let anyone give you a hard time about cargo pants again," Axel replied.

"I couldn't agree more. It's all about functionality," Dr. Green added.

Axel aimed the light, rotating in a circle. The dim light revealed another sarcophagus. Quinn stepped closer and circled all four corners, squinting. "There's something different about this one."

Intricate carvings and symbols etched into its surface were different from the other ones they had encountered. The patterns formed a more cohesive story, depicting ancient figures engaged in a battle against a monstrous creature. Quinn traced his fingers over the grooves, trying to decipher the hidden meaning.

"There's something important about these carvings. Dr. Green, can you see if you can translate any of these symbols?"

Dr. Green squinted and leaned closer, studying them intently. His eyes widened, and then he retrieved the device. Dr. Green pondered for a moment, his brow furrowed. "There are legends surrounding these ancient artifacts. It's said that each sarcophagus contains a relic of immense power. It could be that the beacon is inside here. And this device, one of the figures in the etchings appears to be holding something that looks very similar," he said, touching the side.

As the last words left Dr. Green's lips, a soft light surrounded the sarcophagus. It grew brighter throughout the chamber with each passing second. A pulsating orb flew up from inside before stopping in mid-air, responding to Dr. Green's touch.

"I think we've found it," Quinn whispered. "The beacon. The key to understanding all of this."

"Too bad you won't be alive to discover exactly what it is," a voice in the dark shot out behind them.

The figure aimed his weapon squarely at Quinn and fired.

CHAPTER 12

Tier 1, Earth 2/Multiverse 732, loop 15

AFTER RE-ENTERING THE singularity for the fifteenth time, Quinn spent the next few minutes carefully remembering and following exactly what he'd done just before leaving for the surface successfully in the last loop, including visiting the simulation room. He explained to Sentry what they'd found.

Sentry analyzed the new intel and gave Quinn a quick rundown of the possibilities. Quinn reflected on the possibilities and then activated a few simulations before leaving for the surface. Once they landed, Quinn followed the same actions until they met with Kira's group.

"That's some story," Ubuntu said. Jeremy kept gazing at Kira while occasionally averting his eyes to the side, but a couple of times their eyes locked. When they did, she inspected him a bit closer.

"I believe you," Kira said. Ubuntu's eyes widened, and he glanced back at Kira.

Ubuntu ceded the discussion to Quinn who laid out in more detail the events leading up to his death. He explained the layout as best he remembered and everything Kira might need to avoid getting captured.

Quinn had more to tell, but Ubuntu signaled for them to move if they were to advance ahead of their prior captors. Quinn continued, "I think I might have an idea. In the last loop, I detected a pattern in the singularity's energy fluctuations when we entered Earth's orbit. If we can manipulate those fluctuations, we might be able to disrupt the loop and regain control."

Dr. Green's eyes widened. "How do we do that?"

Quinn took a deep breath. "I learned from Sentry when I first restarted the loop that the device is designed to manipulate quantum energy signatures. If we can get our hands on it, we might have a chance. The only problem is we need to use it with the beacon."

"What about the other version of us?" Jeremy asked.

"My best guess is they're looking for the same thing. And that likely means we're heading in the same direction," he said, pausing, "or at least trying to. So if we are successful, we'll likely run into them. If we don't, we still need to find a way to either shut down the energy field or keep it from activating if we attempt a scan of the surface."

Once they dispensed with the pleasantries and plan of action, they continued to move cautiously through the labyrinthine corridors, following Quinn's recollection of the layout. They encountered a few obstacles, including hidden traps and patrolling guards, but evaded them with a combination of quick thinking and teamwork.

As they approached the chamber where the sarcophagus was located, Quinn's chest tightened. For a moment, his mind got lost in the complex web of the organization. It made him question if it would even be possible to stop them on a larger scale. He wondered if he would simply be putting out little fires from different factions across the multitude of multiverses. He shut the thoughts out of his mind and moved forward with the team.

Once they reached the entrance of the chamber and cautiously stepped inside, the sarcophagus and pulsating orb stole their attention. Quinn inched closer, nearing the crypt. As he did, a voice echoed through the chamber. "So you've made it this far again."

He turned to see who spoke but already recognized the voice. An image retreated into the shadows. A blast of light shot out from the direction where the voice originated and struck Quinn square in the chest, and then another. He fell to the ground with a thud. As he lay on the ground, more bursts of light flew past him and into his companions. He held his eyes open as long as he could and hoped to get a glimpse of his perpetrators, and then his eyes closed shut.

Tier 1, Earth 2, loop 16

After re-entering the singularity, Quinn followed the same path as the prior loop and made his way to the simulation room. He willed his thoughts to the machine and quickly calmed his mind to the lower brainwave frequency needed to communicate directly with Sentry's avatar.

Quinn's consciousness emerged in the familiar simulation room. He blinked, adjusting to the virtual environment. Before him stood Sentry. "This room is so sterile, we can do better than this," Sentry said.

The environment surrounding Quinn faded. In an

instant, the room transformed into an outdoor veranda in the center of a vast lavender field that extended as far as the eye could see. The edge of the field on one side merged with the horizon. On the other, it flowed upward onto rolling hills. Three large banyan trees dotted the field a few hundred yards from the Veranda.

"This is a real place, you know."

Quinn turned to see Sentry sitting slouched in a comfortable position, gazing across the landscape.

"I grew up here on my Earth before my consciousness was transferred. My early childhood was uneventful. And what I didn't know at the time, strangely so. As a teenager, I learned about the hardships many nearby residents faced. And as I grew older, I learned all too well what that often entailed."

Quinn reflected on Sentry's words and let the beacon take a back seat to what Sentry was saying. The field was enticing, and Quinn got a sense that there was a longing for the past.

"What do you mean?"

"Our worlds were very similar up until the fall of the Berlin Wall. Or I should say, the fall in your world. It never fell in ours, more of a crumble that happened gradually after our Balko-Prussian Wars. Something I understand never happened in your time."

Quinn listened intently. Sentry rattled on about the beauty of his hometown, to the point where it became droning, but then the conversation shifted when he got to the point about his parents.

"You see," he said, his voice choking up, "they killed her. I watched helplessly. And what made it worse was they were younger than me. But for whatever reason, I don't know if it was their sheer numbers or something else, but I couldn't stop them. The memory has grown hazy, and even the construct itself can't focus it. These crystals have limitations, and unfortunately, one of them is muting my darkest memories."

He paused for a moment, barely able to keep his voice from cracking. "They killed my mom right in front of me."

A sudden sense of déjà vu overcame Quinn in that instant. "I'm sorry," he said, pausing. "That memory doesn't seem that muted. It's like you're having a visceral, and very normal, reaction to a horrific event."

"There was more, I swear. And it's not just that memory, it's others. It's like I have a skeleton or a shell, but the guts are gone. All I am left with is the frame. This memory just happens to be one of the main support beams, and I don't have that many."

Quinn squinted and pondered Sentry's words. "How exactly did you come to be in your current form?" He paused for a moment before continuing. "Were you forced into it?"

"That's a complex question without an easy answer. The short answer is both. I chose to join the construct as my last resort, faced with the alternative of death due to my circumstances, not the construct's creator. The crystals needed a more cohesive control. And they were failing at the time."

Quinn interrupted. "Who built the crystals?"

"A friend approached me, someone I knew who was trying to find a solution to the impending supernova. He'd been using machine learning to search for an answer. He was so close. The coded frame kept falling apart before it reached a critical threshold. He'd mentioned he thought an upload of an existing consciousness should work, but only if some of the human elements were stripped out to keep it more stable.

Not all of them, mind you, but just enough so you wouldn't have a system that spontaneously developed an anxiety disorder or a God complex."

"And this friend, this was the person responsible for the creation of the construct, the crystals we took from the planet surface during our prior trip?"

"There's a lot you don't know about the construct. What you learned from before is just the beginning. But I can say that it's more than one person. Like most great leaps forward, there are usually numerous people involved. That was the case here, but there always needs to be a foundation. My friend was one of the people who helped lay that foundation. To do so, he had to activate the construct, provide it with an overall intelligence to coordinate its behavior, and do what was needed to save the planet."

Quinn exhaled audibly. "But at a cost."

"One I was willing to pay. I didn't want to, mind you. I'm not suicidal."

"So was this a true upload, a continuity of consciousness or . . ."

"Sadly, it was not. I'm afraid to say that I'm nothing more than a phantom copy of my former self. My muted thoughts recall what my original incarnation felt, but only to the degree required by the construct to work properly. Regardless, it was better to have something of me live on than nothing at all. And while I wasn't looking forward to death, it gave me a sense of comfort at the end."

"Which was what, exactly?"

There was a long pause. "That is a story for another day, but it brings me to the answer you seek. Based on the information I've absorbed from your thoughts, it's clear the powers on the surface are running a parallel loop, just like the one from my home planet by the alt version of you. And if we're lucky, that may give you an advantage. Follow my instructions to the letter," Sentry said.

CHAPTER 13

EARTH 2/MULTIVERSE 732, PLANET SURFACE, LOOP 16

QUINN'S GROUP LANDED at the same spot and at about the same time. Once they buried the shuttle, Quinn informed his team, "I spoke with Sentry, and he shared some important information. It seems that those on the surface are running a separate loop, just like the one we experienced on the planet where we retrieved the construct. If we can leverage this loop, we might have a chance to disrupt the energy fluctuations and regain control."

Dr. Green's eyes widened. "How do we do that?"

Quinn smiled and looked up. "Right on cue."

A second smaller shuttle approached, lowering to just a few feet from the exact spot as the landing party shuttle. It was roughly one-tenth the size of theirs and not large enough to carry a person except for a very small child. The rest of the group eyed the shuttle until it landed.

The moment it did, Quinn opened the hatch. "We do it with these."

"Smart. Very smart," Axel said.

"So you sent them separately so they wouldn't activate the energy field within the shuttle," Dr. Green said.

"There was a chance they'd still activate the energy field, but Sentry suggested that the trigger requires the spheres to be in close enough proximity to something with residual exotic matter when they pass the Lagrangian point. I wasn't sure if it was myself or the exotic matter lining the hull of the larger shuttle that caused it, which is why I sent them separately in the micropod."

Quinn's face hardened. "We need to locate the device that can manipulate the quantum energy signatures. Sentry's given me the layout, and I've practiced it in the simulator. Once we have the device, we'll need to use it with the beacon to create a disruption."

Jeremy spoke up. "What about the other version of us?"

"We'll probably run into them. And even if we don't, we still need to find a way to either shut down the energy field or prevent it from activating when we attempt a scan of the surface."

With the plan laid out, they continued their cautious progress through the labyrinthine corridors. Quinn's memory served as their guide, and they navigated through hidden traps and avoided patrolling guards.

Finally, they reached the chamber with the sarcophagus, which was positioned at the center of the room. An orb gleamed, suspended above it. The room itself was expansive, its walls made of smooth, dark stone that absorbed the light rather than reflected it.

Just as Quinn was about to take another step forward, a voice echoed through the chamber. "So you've made it this far again."

Quinn slipped his hand into his satchel and activated two of the spheres they'd sent in the micropod. Within a fraction of a second, a pocket of space-time radiated outward. Every person in the chamber stopped mid-motion. Quinn approached each member of the team and manually placed their hand on one of the two orbs, each joining Quinn's time bubble once they did.

"What now?" Jeremy asked.

"Sentry believes the beacon's proximity will prevent our annihilation."

"Is this thing the beacon?" Jeremy asked, staring directly at the orb hovering over the sarcophagus.

"That's our best guess."

"And by *our*, you mean you and Sentry?"

"That's it. But now we've got to get the device first to deactivate the beacon. Hopefully, it will be easy with time frozen. The only concern is how far away from it we can travel before the spheres make us vulnerable," Quinn said.

"Why not just leave them here with us? You go find the device," Jeremy said.

"You think that's how we ended up here in the first place? I mean, if Quinn goes running off and dies, we're stuck here to live out our lives, and he gets another do-over. So maybe one of us ends up calling for help, and that's what we find on the video that brought us here in the first place," Axel said.

"Yeah, but Quinn was in the video," Jeremy replied.

"So it might not be Quinn who ends up running off," Axel added.

"Let me just stop you. That's not how this works. We used the spheres to travel not just to a new universe in our multiverse, but to an entirely different multiverse. The versions we're searching for are not us. They didn't branch off from some timeline in our multiverse. They branched off from some timeline in their multiverse, so the laws of causality don't apply since we're from different multiverses altogether."

"So what happens if we die in this multiverse?"

What else is new? Quinn thought to himself.

"It's already happened, many times. We start our timeline from the moment of entry. But I can't go any farther. The holographic universe is distinct for each multiverse, so my timeline in this multiverse formed the moment we entered the singularity. So I can't go back farther than that. Our only way out is to use the spheres to power Tier 1. And I suspect the other version of us is likely trying to do something similar," Quinn said.

"How did they get here? I didn't see any ships. And if they also have spheres, wouldn't they have been destroyed too?" Axel asked.

Quinn thought for a moment. He'd gotten used to answering questions with limited information available to make a reply. It was part guesswork and part hope. Saying things aloud was one of the best ways he'd found to rehash his thoughts and hear what made sense and what didn't. Sometimes it worked, and sometimes was better than never.

"That, I don't know. Maybe they have a way of traveling the multiverse. Maybe they found a method to jump in closer to the beacon. Who knows? I'm sure we'll learn more if and when we find them, and the only way I see us doing that is by successfully getting the device and using it to deactivate the orb," Quinn replied.

Quinn hesitated a moment before leaving. "And if it helps any, I'm the one leaving, so if you still think this has anything to do with the video, that should put your mind at ease. Since I'm the one leaving, that's definitely not us."

Dr. Green stood, holding his chin. "And I'll study the impact of the time bubble in the surrounding area. The beacon might exert a field that impacts space-time as the radius away expands."

"Then you all need to stay with Dr. Green. I don't want any of us to separate."

"What about you?" Axel asked.

Quinn's face dropped. He tried and failed not to reveal it. "Fine. You're right."

"Good. I've got your six, Boss."

"Don't get too far away from the beacon. You should stay on the same path we took to get here so you don't get turned around or run into any traps," Quinn told Dr. Green.

"I wasn't born yesterday," Dr. Green said.

With that, Quinn and Axel went off down a side corridor Quinn had traced out in the simulation room before the trip. As they lurked, Quinn kept his focus on everything in the room. "It should be up on the left and then down the right side. There's another sarcophagus in the room we're looking for, along with a small gap between the wall and the floor. The device should be in the gap. That's where Dr. Green found it the first time."

"Just lead the way."

In the adjacent corridor, Dr. Green and Jeremy strolled off in the opposite direction. "You sure this is such a good idea?" Jeremy asked.

"What? Studying the time bubble?"

"Leaving the beacon. If the time bubble does break down

with distance, we might end up dead. If Quinn dies, he gets a do-over. If we die, that's it."

"Ah, that's where you're wrong. This beacon here, and this sarcophagus, are creating a parallel time bubble. This might not be the only one. My theory is that The Way uses the spheres to create time bubbles in controlled areas."

Jeremy's eyes widened. "So you think if we die, we will end up in a time loop with everyone else?"

"Essentially, yes."

"How does that give them an advantage?"

"What do you mean?"

"Well, if everyone is in the time loop, then won't everyone within the time loop benefit from the same knowledge, which would thwart the plan?" Jeremy asked.

Dr. Green thought for a moment. "Maybe. Or it could be that there is some technique to target or select who would relive the time loop."

Jeremy's brow furrowed. "This doesn't make sense to me."

"It doesn't have to. What I can say is that I'm not certain we will die our final death, or at least this version of ourselves will die the final death. I think there is a great possibility that we will relive the loop."

"But from what starting point? When we emerge from the singularity?"

"That's one possibility. Another is from the activation of the loop by the sarcophagus."

Dr. Green and Jeremy debated the theory until Jeremy, facing the prospect of a death loop or a final demise, grew apathetic. With no certainty in preventing a supernova through a planetary array, he figured he might as well risk it, given his lack of options.

Once Jeremy shut up, Dr. Green resumed his analysis of the area, inspecting the fine dust particles in the air to see if there was any motion. There wasn't any. The insects were also immobile. He put a small object on the ground to measure tiny tremors that would indicate any geological activity.

"I'm not feeling anything from below the surface, so I think the bubble extends around a very large area, even beyond the planet."

Quinn located the chamber where Dr. Green originally located the device. In front of him, bathed in the flickering torchlight, a baroque golden sarcophagus emerged with intricate engravings of ancient images of gods and pharaohs. As he drew closer, the ornate surface painted fleeting patterns upon the walls. Axel kept watch in the other direction.

Quinn dropped to the floor near the closest wall. "The gap is right here, so the device should be somewhere nearby."

His eyes scanned both directions. "I think I see something," he said, shifting to the right. "Got it."

Quinn stood up and revealed the small, rectangular device they'd been looking for. "You think these two tombs work together?" Axel asked.

Something rustled to the left of them. Axel and Quinn turned toward the entrance. Both their eyes widened. Standing before them was a man who was the spitting image of Quinn along with Dr. Green.

"Thank God! We weren't sure if you made it," Alternate Quinn said.

A third person pushed his way through from behind them. He sported a slick EverQuest IV T-shirt and cutoff jean shorts with a bulging muscled physique and long hair like a frontman for a classic rock group in a parallel universe.

Quinn smiled. "Gary!"

It took Quinn a moment to stop smiling. Eventually, he added, "We've got a lot of questions."

"And we'll do our best to answer all of them, but we need to leave, and fast."

CHAPTER 14

Planet surface, Earth 2/Multiverse 732, the Great Pyramid

DR. GREEN ADVANCED THROUGH the corridor in front of them until they retraced half the distance of their initial journey.

"Find anything interesting?" Jeremy asked.

"So far everything is as it should. I haven't found anything that brings us closer to any answers, but at least things are functioning as expected."

Jeremy turned the corner and caught an image on the right side of a room they had just entered. He motioned Dr. Green to stop. Dr. Green opened his mouth to speak, but Jeremy put his hand over his mouth and whispered, "Someone's in the other room."

Jeremy slowly bent down until his head was a few inches off the ground and peered into the other room. He retreated and whispered again. "It's a young woman. She's tied up, and two men are watching her."

Dr. Green shook his head and then motioned Jeremy

to follow him in the other direction. When they'd traveled two more corridors, Dr. Green spoke, but still quietly. "So I was right. We're not the only people moving in the bubble. Those working for The Way must have some type of device that keeps them from being affected. We need to find Quinn and Axel."

"What about the girl?"

"She's not our problem. And if you notice, she wasn't frozen either, so maybe she's part of their organization."

"Did you not hear the part about her being tied up?"

Approaching footsteps interrupted them. Dr. Green signaled for Jeremy to move in the other direction. As the marching intensified, they quickly retreated towards the beacon. "Almost there," Dr. Green whispered.

They eyed for an escape route, trying to breathe softly and move silently.

"Two corridors down, there was a small cubicle pedestal. It's not large enough to completely cover both of us, but if we hurry, it could give us enough cover to allow us to remain hidden from whoever is coming as they pass by."

Dr. Green strode toward their original position near the beacon. The steps in the distance grew louder, and both soon increased their pace to a quick jog, careful to make as little noise as possible.

"There," Dr. Green whispered. He yanked Jeremy behind him as they threw themselves down just as footsteps were upon them. They placed their backs against the pedestal away from the entrance and faced the opposing wall.

For a moment, the patter of feet stopped. Dr. Green and Jeremy froze and held their breath like they were the main characters in a horror movie with the killer just inches away.

Voices echoed from beyond the entrance. Neither could make out the language the figures spoke, but they kept motionless until the footsteps resumed.

More steps from the opposing direction grew louder until both sets stopped again. Dr. Green assumed they must've been members of the same party meeting up. They waited a couple more minutes until the patter faded completely.

"I think they're gone," Jeremy said.

"We should return to the sarcophagus and wait for Quinn," Dr. Green replied.

Jeremy glanced in both directions and headed in the direction of the beacon.

A few corridors down, Quinn stood face-to-face with the other version of him, each duo mirroring the other's appearance and demeanor. Two sets of identical features stared at each other.

The versions of Quinn and Dr. Green from what Quinn assumed was the video stepped forward. Quinn extended a hand toward his counterpart. "We need to deactivate the beacon. It's causing the time loop and keeping us trapped here. We've located the device that controls it, and we're here to help you retrieve it."

Alternate Quinn and Dr. Green continued their conversations a short while longer, going into the details of some of the trouble they encountered and more specifics on why they were there and why they sent the video. Once alternate Quinn explained what he thought was important, Quinn signaled for them to move.

They weaved through the corridors, their strides echoing softly in the frozen silence. Finally, they arrived at the parallel path, and Quinn signaled for everyone to halt. He peered around the corner, scanning for any signs of danger. Satisfied that the coast was clear, he motioned for the others to follow. As they continued their journey, marching echoed toward them.

"Someone's coming," Quinn said.

The four of them quickly withdrew and pressed their bodies flat against the wall away from the entrance. The earthy aroma of dirt filled Quinn's nose. It reminded him of a simpler time when he was four or five years old, curious and sniffing at the soil while he picked through the roly-polies and small critters that flitted through the grains of moist dirt.

The steps grew louder for several seconds until finally, they receded in the background.

"We should return to the sarcophagus. Jeremy and Dr. Green will be waiting for us. Then we can decide what to do next," Quinn said.

The alternate version of Dr. Green agreed, and they quickly headed toward the sarcophagus housing the beacon. Flames crackled from torches housed in wooden stands near the top of the walls. Hieroglyphics decorated the sandstone, and particles of sand swirled around them as they hurried to find it.

Quinn coughed as the intense smoke stung his eyes and clouded his sight. The tight space, crowded with four people like sardines in a can, amplified the fumes. He quickly covered his nose with a handkerchief and trailed his companions down the narrow corridor.

They continued until the passageway opened to a larger one and headed toward the tomb. The alternate Dr. Green stalled briefly, brushing his fingers over the grooves as if searching for something.

The earth rumbled, and dust rattled to the floor. Quinn covered his eyes and coughed. All four of them covered their faces with cloth and continued, quickening their pace.

"We made it," Jeremy said.

"Let's just hope the others make it too," Dr. Green replied.

They surveyed the room and inspected for any changes from the recent quakes, but the circular room holding the sarcophagus remained unfazed.

Dr. Green observed the golden hue of the coffin within the sarcophagus. Jewels were dangling off the edges. A large gold key with three loops rested near the top of it. The loops had rubies inside, and the torches caused them to glitter. He squinted, inspecting it closer.

"There's a small opening underneath the key's teeth. It looks like a good fit for the device, assuming Quinn and Axel were able to find it," Dr. Green said.

"Let's just hope they didn't get captured. Maybe then we'll find out."

Just then, several people entered the room. Dr. Green stared at a mirror image of himself except for the clothes. Both had floppy, unkempt, graying hair that made them look like mad scientists.

"So I see you've met yourselves. Now let's get on with this," Gary said.

"Get on with what, exactly?" Jeremy asked.

"Isn't it obvious? We sent you a message we weren't sure you would get. Now you're here. All you have to do now is take us to Tier 1 and then drop us off using the spheres," Gary replied.

The original Dr. Green exhaled. "There's only one problem with that. We can't, at least not yet. We can't seem to get past the people pacing, for starters. And then there's the issue of the beacon we need to shut down."

"Come on, man. That was implied," Gary said.

Jeremy rolled his eyes. "Looks like you're the same in every universe."

"Every multiverse," the alternate Dr. Green corrected.

"Does someone have the remote to shut this thing off?" Jeremy asked.

Alternate Dr. Green lifted up his hand, holding up the rectangular device. "Got it right here. There's only one problem. Once we activate this, every guard is going to be headed this way, and they all have special shielding that prevents them from being frozen in time bubbles. Our weapons aren't exactly the greatest, so we're going to need to get to your transport before they can catch us."

"Or knock them out," Axel added.

Everyone in the group except for Axel crowded around the sarcophagus, inspecting it. Axel stood watch at the entrance, his palm clenched around a borrowed laser pistol from the alternate group. Up ahead, the march of footsteps coincided with the appearance of the heavily armored and weapon-clad guards.

"Guys," Axel whispered. "They're here."

CHAPTER 15

EARTH 2/MULTIVERSE 732, PLANET SURFACE, BY THE BEACON

JEREMY TOOK UP position out of sight and directly behind the sarcophagus opposite the door. Quinn and Dr. Green stood adjacent to him. Gary and the alternate Dr. Green flanked them on both sides and were the most visible to anyone who might enter.

"Any ideas?" Jeremy said.

"Yeah, stay quiet," Gary replied.

The footsteps grew louder, and Axel slid sideways and flattened himself near the entrance but held a firm grip on the laser pistol. Gary and alternate Dr. Green crouched lower in a pathetic fighting pose.

The guards closed in, and Quinn's heart rate jumped. He braced himself for the possibility of another reset, but the marching steps receded once the guards passed the entrance, moving farther left until they vanished altogether.

Everyone stood still for the next minute until finally,

alternate Dr. Green broke the silence. "I think they're gone for now. We don't have much time."

"What about the rest of your group?" Quinn asked.

"They'll find their way here. They always do," alternate Dr. Green replied.

Quinn's eyes widened. "So you've been looping too? For how long?"

"Since we entered the singularity."

"Why and how did you enter without a transport ship?" Quinn paused for a moment and then added, "And why did you call us?"

"Do you remember when saboteurs nearly destroyed the array?" alternate Dr. Green asked.

"Of course," Quinn replied.

Footsteps interrupted them. Standing at the door, alternate Quinn entered. The Quinns stared at each other, their green eyes identical. They stepped closer. Quinn squinted. Alternate Quinn smiled.

Behind him, alternate Jeremy strode ahead. The room now held eight people, three pairs of nearly identical copies plus Axel and Gary, who eyed each other up and down.

"So I just want to be clear here. You sent us the message on the video," Quinn said to alternate Quinn.

"We did, yes. And I'm sure as my Dr. Green has probably already said to you, we're stuck here. We need to hitch a ride with you," alternate Quinn said.

"What happened to your array segment or ship?" Quinn asked.

"A long story."

"Why did you come?"

"We came for the same reason you did, to stop The Way.

Or at least throw a monkey wrench in their plans. The ones closest to home anyway," alternate Quinn replied.

"But why this planet? Why this time, this multiverse?"

Alternate Quinn exhaled. His face fell. "Because freedom isn't free. Because even though I could relive my life over and over again with some degree of certainty, the rest of our universes don't share the same fate. And to the second part of your question, the data led us here."

"And when you say *our universes*, what do you mean exactly?"

"We are from the same multiverse. We are also from almost the same timeline, but in your timeline, your Tier 1 got tossed into a parallel universe. In mine, I got propelled into my father's body and landed in 1984. When I returned, I didn't make it all the way, and I lived in an alternate timeline for the last five years leading up to the event. So we share the same memories up until the point where you entered the wormhole, but I have extra," alternate Quinn replied.

CHAPTER 16

EARTH 2/MULTIVERSE 732, PLANET SURFACE, LOOP 16

FOR THE NEXT several minutes, the duplicate teams discussed key differences in their timelines and what needed to happen before they could leave the surface. And then they got to events after they arrived.

"What about the woman? Are we going to leave her tied up?" Jeremy asked.

"One thing at a time. Until we stop the beacon, we're not in a position to help ourselves first. And if we can't help ourselves, we can't help anyone else," Dr. Green said.

"So who has the device? Dr. Green thinks the slot in the key teeth on the sarcophagus holds the device."

"Sounds like a very smart man," alternate Dr. Green said. Just then, he placed his hand in his pocket and retrieved the rectangular gadget. "I had to wait until we were all here. What I discovered from the hieroglyphs suggests a bubble within a bubble will form once I enter the key."

"Bubble within a bubble?" Jeremy said.

"Bubble within a bubble within a loop," alternate

Dr. Green said and then paused. "The Way rigged the planet, which I'm sure you already know, to detect exotic matter with a specific signature. It also has the effect of creating a time loop for anyone in the area."

"Then how come we can't remember it?" Jeremy asked.

"Both Quinns can because they have a mental time travel ability due to their dark matter residue. But The Way has technology that allows them to remember as well," alternate Dr. Green replied.

"So how does that work? Is it the same consciousness or just a different branch in the timeline?" Jeremy asked.

"For those protected, their mind returns to the beginning of the bubble, but for everyone else, they continue beyond the loop. Essentially, it lets anyone who dies that is protected go to the beginning of the loop until they get the desired outcome."

Jeremy's expression suggested he was digesting the information. "So in other words, the bad guys along with both Quinns get thrown to some point in the past, but we die in this timeline if we die right now."

"That about sums it up," alternate Quinn said.

"Well that sucks."

"According to Quinn, that's already happened many times."

"Maybe so, but I don't want it happening again."

"I may have a solution for that," alternate Dr. Green said.

Jeremy's eyes widened. "There's a portal somewhere nearby. I haven't been able to find it. It's laced with exotic matter. It's essentially a double wormhole separated by only a few meters in the same room. I suspect this creates residual exotic matter that will cling to your body and allow you to stay in the loop."

"So we'll be like Quinn?"

"From what I've been able to find, those who pass through the loop still need to wear the tech, which measures how much exotic matter they have left remaining and how many loops they can travel. If we can find the portal, it should work even if we can't find the measuring device," alternate Dr. Green said.

Both Quinns listened. "So I think what we need to do then is clear. Destroy the portals, deactivate the beacon, and then escape the planet. We'll drop you guys off, and then we'll head to our home timeline. If we can find one of those measurement devices, that will be a plus. We've been looking for a way to determine how much residual dark matter I have left to loop. Maybe we can reverse engineer and create the measurement devices on demand," Quinn said.

"That's exactly what I was thinking," alternate Quinn added.

Axel interrupted, "I don't want to break up this family reunion, but we've got company."

Marching accompanied by the chatter of an unknown language echoed from the adjacent corridor. Quinn half expected the footsteps to pass like they'd done that last couple of times, but they grew louder.

A group of six guards and two other men dressed in robes entered the chamber. A few of them spoke loudly in some unintelligible language.

Axel aimed the laser gun squarely at two of the guards. He was about to fire, but one of the robed men spoke. "I wouldn't do that if I were you. You're vastly outnumbered, and you don't want to piss them off," he said.

Axel looked for confirmation from Quinn, whose eyes told him to stand down. "Any chance we could just walk out of here?" Quinn asked.

The robed man forced a smile. Lines creased his forehead, and a short gray cropped haircut accentuated his slick yet mature appearance. "Why don't you start by telling us why you are here."

"Funny thing you should ask. We were looking for some friends, and whaddya know, we found 'em. So if you don't mind, I think we'll just head on out," Quinn said.

Quinn strode toward the exit, and his companions lined up behind him. Four guards quickly moved to block the exit. The robed man's face transformed into one more severe. "I do admire your audacity, in whatever form you take, Quinn—" he paused and turned toward Quinn's double "—and Quinn," he finished.

"Wonderful. Then you won't mind if we leave."

The remaining two guards moved from the outside in, further blocking the group's path.

"You have to know this is your end. We are not letting you go. You and your duplicates won't ever leave here. And this was by design. The beauty of it is, you don't even know it or understand why," the robed man said.

"Then why don't you tell us?" Quinn asked.

"This isn't some movie where I tell you all my dirty little secrets just because you ask. This is the real world, and this is where you die."

The guards stepped forward, restricting the group's position. Axel aimed his laser pistol, releasing a short burst of energy into the robed man's face, who shrieked and mumbled something akin to a growl as he fell to his knees. "Whatever you say bounces off of me and sticks to you," Axel replied to the man's unintelligible words.

Quinn and Jeremy followed suit, each firing their laser pistols at the guards. The six well-muscled men moved to the side and shot back. Jeremy grunted. "You alright, man?" Axel asked.

Everyone kept firing. "Not alright. Just got shot in my ass."

"Just be thankful it wasn't the other side," Axel replied.

Energy bolts zinged back and forth, reflecting off the chamber's walls. Axel swung his laser pistol around, finding his mark on another guard's shoulder. The guard grimaced, dropped his weapon, and then scowled toward Axel.

Quinn pulled out a small grenade and tossed it into the air. It erupted into a brilliant flash, blinding the remaining guards momentarily.

Dr. Green moved in front of alternate Dr. Green and shot wildly at the guard who had just struck Jeremy. Alternate Dr. Green dropped to the position of the key slot on the sarcophagus and slid the device into position. The device stopped short halfway in, followed by a loud click. For a moment, nothing happened. A fraction of a second later, the entire chamber shook.

"You didn't think it would be that easy, did you?" the other unharmed robed man said.

The guards retreated and pulled their injured companion behind the entrance into the adjacent corridor. Once they were out completely, the ground shook. "Hey, guys, we better move," Axel said.

From behind the closing walls, the guards fired a volley of shots toward them. Axel returned fire, dodging and moving forward. The others rushed toward the front entrance. Something groaned from behind Quinn. He ignored it and joined Axel in firing. A burst of wind blew past them, and then the walls shut. A lamp light flickered, and then everything went black.

"This isn't good," one of the Jeremys said in the dark. Quinn couldn't tell which one.

"This isn't good? No shit. I thought you were supposed to be the smart one. Which one of you is that anyway?" Axel said, unable to clearly see which Jeremy spoke from the shadows.

"Is everyone okay?" Quinn asked.

"I got grazed on my right arm, but it's just a flesh wound," one of the Dr. Greens said.

"Which one of you is that?"

"The one with a transport," alternate Dr. Green replied.

"We'll find a way out of this," Quinn replied.

"I'm not so sure about that. This was a trap from the beginning. They wanted us to come here, wanted both groups to come here. Who knows how many others they've lured here too."

Quinn remained silent, willing his eyes to adapt to the dimming light. The sarcophagus had dimmed to a faint orange pulse, cycling every two seconds.

A light appeared from Axel's phone. He shone it on the lamps, now extinguished from the burst of wind. "Anyone got a light?"

"Almost no one smokes anymore, so I think you're out of luck," Axel replied.

"I'll settle for a flashlight."

A couple more phone lights turned on, one focused and one diffuse, lighting the chamber enough to see the surroundings. A faint cloud of dust continued to settle toward the ground, and a musty odor filled the room.

Quinn exhaled and took a brief moment to gather his thoughts. Suddenly, the roof lowered from above, followed by a low rumble.

"Uh, guys. Another problem. Any ideas on how to get out of here?" Jeremy asked.

Both Dr. Greens looked up, inspecting the ceiling and looking down at the sarcophagus. "I don't think we're getting out of this one," Dr. Green said.

Axel rushed over and shot his laser pistol at the sphere hovering above the sarcophagus. The silver ball absorbed the light with no other visible impacts. He fired again. The same thing happened. Jeremy joined in the firing and then alternate Jeremy. The sphere didn't change, but the room lit up from the frequent laser bursts being continually discharged into the sphere.

The roof closed a third of the way down. Axel shifted his firing to the pedestal. The others soon followed. A few chips of sandstone shot out from the impact, but the pedestal remained intact.

Jeremy grabbed the sphere with his hands, but the sphere remained floating over the sarcophagus. The ceiling continued dropping and reached the halfway point. Once it did, the eyes of the sarcophagus changed to bright green.

"Guys, something's happening," Jeremy said.

Alternate Dr. Green slid the device into the keyhole and then removed it. The ceiling kept dropping. He tried again.

The ceiling plunged to around one meter above the ground. Everyone fell to their knees firing. Jeremy shifted his aim to the corners of the room.

"It's been good knowing you, but I guess this is how it ends," Jeremy said.

CHAPTER 17

Tier 1, Earth 2/Multiverse 732, loop 17

AFTER RE-ENTERING THE singularity, Quinn followed the same path as the prior loop and made his way to the simulation room. He willed his thoughts to the machine and quickly calmed his mind to achieve the lowered brainwave frequency needed to communicate directly with Sentry's avatar.

Quinn's consciousness emerged in the familiar simulation room. He blinked, adjusting to the environment. Before him stood Sentry. "So it was a trap," Sentry said.

The environment surrounding Quinn faded. In an instant, the room transformed into the same outdoor veranda in a vast lavender field as the prior loop. Sentry sat slouched, gazing across the landscape.

"Things don't always turn out the way you expect them to. But despite the snare they've set for you, and I'm guessing other versions of you as well, you are still on equal footing whether you realize it or not. That may not be the case for your friends who are all dead now in their timeline, but there's nothing you can do about that. Let's focus on this one. Follow my instructions to the letter," Sentry said.

A short while later, Quinn's group landed at the same spot at about the same time. Once they buried the shuttle, Quinn reflected on the new revelations he'd gotten from Sentry.

Quinn smiled and looked up. "Right on cue."

A smaller pod, one-tenth the size of their shuttle, descended and settled feet from their position. The group watched closely until it landed, after which Quinn immediately opened the hatch. "We do it with these," he said, holding a couple of spheres.

"Smart. Very smart," Axel replied.

"You sent them separately so they wouldn't activate the energy field within the shuttle?" Dr. Green said.

"That's not the only thing we need to do. The beacon is an ambush, but we still have to find it again. We can't use them here. We need to be close enough to use the spheres without the energy field activating. And even when we manage to do that, others may still be able to move freely in the frozen time bubble."

Axel's brow furrowed. "Then what use are they if the guys who are going to come after us are immune?"

Quinn secured the spheres from the micro-transport, stashed them in his satchel, and then surveyed the area ahead.

"What we discovered is that not all The Way's forces are immune. They must be actively sent through the special portal, which is costly, so only the highest-level guards and active members are in the loop. The exotic particles get depleted with each person who walks through. That alone gives us a better advantage. But that's not the only thing. It may be possible to use the spheres in such a way that no one is immune except those within a certain radius."

"And how do you plan on doing that?" Axel replied.

"With the help of us from another timeline, of course," Quinn replied.

Quinn set about mapping the terrain and gave the rundown of the locations where they could expect guards. They also had a rough idea of which area they would find alternate Quinn's team. He then laid out the plan to evade the guards, meet up with their alternate selves, modify the spheres, and deactivate the beacon. It would be a juggling act, but if they followed the plan closely and watched their time, they should be able to perform it before they inadvertently alerted The Way.

"The entryway is here," Quinn said. Dr. Green and Jeremy strode toward the Great Pyramid base away from their buried shuttle. Axel kept his hands on his pistol, ready to fire. Jeremy jogged along, and Dr. Green kept pace but just barely.

Quinn didn't notice any differences before entering the pyramid in his last loops, aside from the speed and missing Ubuntu's group because of it, and he considered how they might play a role in destroying the beacon. He left out some of the details regarding Ubuntu out of expediency.

When they approached the entrance, Quinn cleared the ground to the hidden passage and lifted the boards concealed under fine dust. "Their base is under here, the group I told you about."

Quinn jogged down a series of short stairwells that led to their large underground bunker. Once they arrived, several dozen men blocked Quinn's path. "Who are you?" Ubuntu asked.

Quinn spent the next ten minutes explaining the last dozen time loops and what he thought they needed to do to destroy the beacon and return home. He discussed the guards, the trap, and the chambers holding what they thought was the beacon, and described them in great detail.

Ubuntu listened. Kira stepped forward. "We have a common enemy," she said.

"And what can you tell us of this enemy?" Axel asked.

"They are terrible. They've taken everything we had, and they still want more," she added.

"What do they want?" Dr. Green added.

Ubuntu interrupted, "They want to end worlds. As to why, I cannot say. All I know is that they're using this world—" he paused "—our world, to bring about the end of others."

"The beacon," Axel said.

"Yes. I believe that is what you speak of, but it's dangerous."

The moment Ubuntu spoke those words, the faces in his group dropped. He continued, "Our world changed. Pieces of our world vanished until there was almost nothing left. Our world was once like yours, but this beacon has brought back our past, one long forgotten."

Quinn explained their prior predicament as well as what happened the first time they worked together. He also briefly discussed their plan to avoid the prior mistakes.

"In the other loop, you mentioned you'd seen another version of me. We must find and meet up before we can destroy the beacon. The last time we met, we followed your path but were captured. Is there another way to enter underneath the pyramid?" Quinn asked.

Kira exhaled. "There is, but it's even more dangerous.

The rulers here have large, unnatural animals they unleash when they lose control."

Jeremy's eyes widened. "What do you mean, unnatural?"

Ubuntu cut in, "Creatures that are a cross between tigers and birds. Others are combinations of horses and boar. Some told stories of labs where they make herds of fighting beasts. Only one person has survived to tell the tale, but we've seen the animals. A few miles beyond the smallest pyramid, they have a stronghold. Based on what you said, I would imagine your mirror copies could have intended to see what was going on there. There is an entrance halfway between the outpost and the small pyramid."

"Can you show us?" Quinn asked.

Ubuntu lowered his head, and an expression of dread overtook him. "I can take you," Kira replied.

Ubuntu's head jerked up as his eyes met Kira's. She gave him a look that prevented him from speaking. "It's fine. I've been close to the area many times, and I know the way. It will be dangerous, and we could very well see one of the wild animals they use to guard the area."

"We have weapons," Axel said.

"We've used all manner of weapons against them. As I said, they are unnatural and hard to kill, designed specifically, we suspect, with people like you in mind," Ubuntu replied.

Quinn thanked Kira. Despite Ubuntu's cautious warnings, she and several daring clan members joined the group. Ubuntu, apologizing for staying behind, cited his duty to safeguard the rest. Just as they were set to leave, he stopped them.

Ubuntu reached into his pocket and retrieved an object hidden within a handmade felt-like cloth. "Here. It is only one of two that I know exist, and it may prove the deciding factor in your quest," he said. Quinn twisted to turn away, but Ubuntu continued, "But don't open it until you have no choice but to use it. That will make all the difference," he added.

Jeremy and Axel frowned subtly. Quinn suspected they were skeptical and impatient. Dr. Green remained stoic. "Thank you," Quinn replied.

"It's this way," Kira said, her arms stretched and pointed away from the Great Pyramid and toward the Pyramid of Menkaure, the smallest of the three.

Just on looks alone, Quinn wondered what beasts could be hidden within, behind, or underneath. So far, the pyramids themselves had interiors of mostly rock and stone with just a few chambers and corridors that contained not much of anything.

Quinn followed. Tension was evident on everyone's face. Quinn's group held their hands by their pistols, and Kira marched ahead, eyeing the ground as they strode forward.

"So how long ago did you see these creatures you mentioned?" Jeremy asked.

"Not that long, days perhaps. And the sightings are frequent. Every so often, a herd of different animals will stampede the area, beasts of different sorts, both on land and in the sky."

"In the sky?" Jeremy repeated.

Quinn considered her words and wondered if there was any connection to the dinosaur-like animals they'd encountered on the prior planet or if these were completely different.

"Have you seen a pattern to their appearance?" Dr. Green asked.

"They are attracted to movement in the area, the place where you want to go."

"How large is the underground encampment where your people live? Have you spotted them there too?" Dr. Green said.

"There is a great partition below, several hundred paces beyond the boundary of the Great Pyramid. We stay on the other side of it whenever possible. Occasionally the animals will venture beyond it, but usually, that is only after someone goes astray beyond the boundary on the surface. But I've witnessed numerous herds stampeding on many days with no activity from our people," Kira replied.

For the next twenty minutes, they strode along and eyed the horizon. Quinn mentally replayed as much of the prior loops as he remembered and took note of the terrain as they continued.

Quinn stopped, scanning the horizon and falling a few steps behind the group. He resumed his forward motion and then stopped again, twisting a full 360.

"You okay, Boss?" Axel said.

Quinn squinted. "Do you hear that?"

He stood motionless and then slowly spun around again. "Can you hear me now?" a voice finally asked clearly.

"Hear what?" Axel replied.

"Testing, testing. Can you hear me?" the voice asked.

"This is Sentry. Don't say another word if you can hear me. I don't want anyone else to know," a voice said in Quinn's ear.

The ground trembled, softly at first and then violently. Quinn dropped to his knees and placed his hands on the ground.

"It's a stampede! Split in opposite directions to give them

more than one target, and run around them in circles if they get near you. It will confuse them," Kira said.

"They're coming," Quinn said.

"I know. That's why I'm contacting you now," Sentry said in Quinn's ear.

"How is this possible?" Quinn asked.

Kira squinted. "I've explained what I know," Kira replied.

"I realize what you're thinking," Sentry said.

Near the horizon, dark dots emerged. Soon a small cloud of smoke surrounded them, and the dots grew in size and number.

"You're thinking that my protocols are supposed to prevent me from contacting anyone outside the confines of the construct," Sentry added.

What Quinn was actually thinking was how the hell he was going to get out of there in time.

"Should we be moving somewhere away from the approaching herd of creatures?" Jeremy asked.

"Where should we go?" Quinn said.

"I asked first," Jeremy said.

"That's a great question. Run as fast as you can toward Menkaure. My data says that will give you the greatest chance of survival," Sentry replied in Quinn's ear.

"What about the spheres?" Quinn asked.

"My data indicates a 92 percent probability they will trigger an energy bubble if you use them this far away from the beacon. You'll need to be much closer before you can activate it."

"Yeah, I was thinking the same thing. Let's use the spheres," Jeremy replied to Quinn.

"Uh, no. That's not what I meant."

"What did you mean?" Jeremy replied.

Quinn struggled to follow the conversation and avoid revealing Sentry's updated communications to the team.

"Maybe we can activate them remotely using the micro-shuttle," Quinn said.

Axel and Dr. Green gave Quinn puzzled expressions.

"That could work. But we have no way that I know of to remotely activate them," Dr. Green said.

"Whatever you do, better step on it. Those things are only getting closer," Axel added.

The creatures came more into view. Quinn made out at least three different species. One resembled a giant horned giraffe with armor plating. They marched in the center, towering over the other species on either side. On the left, animals similar to a cross between giant porcupines and wild boars stampeded ahead of the mutant giraffes.

The beasts on the right swarmed at breakneck speed. They'd already closed half the distance and would arrive in under a minute. The creatures appeared as a mix of double-headed lions and oversized saber tooth tigers, something Quinn thought might be in the book of Revelations.

"There's no time for that. They're almost here. We only have one possible way to survive," Kira said.

"And what's that?" Jeremy asked.

"Follow me."

CHAPTER 18

Planet surface, Earth 2, loop 17

KIRA RAN LEFT. The group followed but fell dozens of meters behind. Once Quinn put in enough distance between each member of the group, he asked, "Where is she taking us, Sentry?"

"I can send another micro-shuttle and have it to your location in under a minute."

"That won't be enough time."

"Quinn, I've analyzed the data, and I think I can use a modified radio signal to create an identical vibrational frequency to activate the spheres. It's a similar mechanism to what I used to get around my construct restriction. I'd need to convert the radio frequency into sound waves, but the unique nature of the spheres will make that easy. I'm not certain it will work, but there is a better-than-even chance it will. The only thing is that once I activate them, you won't be able to use them, so you'll need to find another method to stop The Way," Sentry said in Quinn's ear.

"No. If we do that, they'll be ready for us in the next

loop. I'd rather die and do it over again. Let's see how Kira's escape plan works and save the spheres as long as possible."

Kira halted and dropped to her knees, lifting up a camouflaged wood-and-cloth hatch revealing an underground passage. Quinn followed, as did the rest of the group. Kira strode deeper. The cover closed, and torches on earthen walls revealed a maze of catacombs.

"This doesn't go all the way to where you said you need to go, but it goes close. If you follow me, I can get you several hundred yards closer, but you'll still be a couple hundred yards shy."

Quinn smiled. "Thank you. I know you've risked a lot bringing us down here."

"Won't they realize what happened and start searching nearby?" Jeremy asked.

"The creatures are vicious, but not that smart. And we were too far away for any of the men hunting us to see clearly. The entrances we have are too well hidden for the beasts to find. And even if they realized it, it would take forever just to find one of the entrances."

Quinn stopped and allowed himself the time to catch his breath, as did the rest of his team. Kira appeared unfazed. As Quinn's breath slowed, his eyes adjusted to the light, and the intricate underground walls came into focus.

Rows and rows of skulls lined earthen shelves that stretched dozens of yards. Strange objects stacked in intricate patterns separated piles of bones that lay strewn across corners as far as the walls extended. Quinn feared disturbing the bone pile might cause an avalanche.

"A bit morbid, don't you think?" Axel said.

"We've reclaimed this wasteland from those chasing us.

They abandoned it long ago after a great plague nearly wiped them out."

Jeremy coughed, choking on his breath. "Plague?" he finally said.

"Don't worry. They genetically engineered the pathogen for rapid action and had a kill switch for decay within weeks. What they didn't anticipate was accidentally bringing it with them, so they left in a rush and never returned. It's safe now, but they chose not to risk it at the time due to its airborne and contact transmission."

She strode deeper into the catacombs. Roughly every fifty yards, more chambers branched off, perpendicular to the entrance corridor, and faded into darkness.

"What else do you have in this place?" Quinn asked.

"I hope you understand I took a great risk bringing you here, and not just to me but to my people. I'm not ready to give away all our secrets, but what I can say is that hopefully, we have a few unexpected things that might turn the battle in our favor if it came to that," she said.

A second later, Kira stopped. A large, hooded figure blocked her path. Quinn recognized it as one of the figures he'd encountered in the first couple of time loops on the surface.

"You don't think we were that stupid to abandon this place, do you? This was all by design."

Dr. Green's eyes made contact with Quinn, who shook his head.

"Quinn, can you hear me?" Sentry said.

Quinn mumbled, "Mm-hmm."

"Great. I've calculated that if you use the spheres at this range, you have a 51 percent probability of not setting off the energy field."

Quinn analyzed the idea. At first, he was confused based on the distance, since they were farther away. But then he realized the data likely had to do with the proximity of the men currently confronting them.

"Mm-mm," Quinn mumbled again.

Three guards approached from behind and struck Kira in the back of the head. Immediately she went limp and fell to the floor. Jeremy groaned and then drew his side pistol. Another guard shot his arm. He cried out, holding the injured hand with the other, and grimaced.

Axel got off a shot and aimed it squarely in the face of the guard who fired on Jeremy. The guard fell to the floor. He shot two more times and then moved to shoot another. Dr. Green joined in on the action and shot another guard nearby. In quick succession, Quinn and Dr. Green fired at the other guards. Within a second, all guards were down on the ground, and only the robed man remained standing.

"You think I care about them?" the robed man said.

Axel shot him in the face, and he went down too. Jeremy rushed to Kira, who still rested unconscious on the floor.

"Or you can do it that way," Sentry said in Quinn's ear.

Jeremy nudged Kira a few times. Finally, she moved. He let out a big breath. "You're alive."

Her eyes opened a smidge. "We have to stop them."

Jeremy turned to the robed man and fired. The rest joined in. He stood, uninjured. Each time the laser came within a short distance from the robe, it shimmered and vanished.

"I've made some more modifications to the transmission signal I'm using to contact you. While your cortical implant may not be actively running, it is possible to use it to passively scan what you're seeing and relay that information to me through radio signals. And from what I can see, you won't be able to kill that man you're currently shooting," Sentry said to Quinn.

"How do we stop him?" Quinn asked.

Axel and Dr. Green kept firing. Jeremy stayed hovering over Kira as she came to.

"You can't stop me," the robed man said.

After speaking, he tapped something on his left arm, which emitted a shimmering light. Quinn's vision went black. A sharp pain struck the back of his head, and soreness engulfed his muscles. He found his palms on cold dirt, his body sprawled on the ground.

Once the ringing in Quinn's ears faded, he pushed himself into a sitting position, opening his eyes to red-and-black patterns that slowly cleared along with his pounding headache. He finally stood and found Kira missing. Jeremy was clutching his arm on the ground from an apparent pistol wound. Axel was already standing. "How bad are you hurt?" Quinn asked Jeremy.

Axel and Dr. Green helped Jeremy to his feet. "It hurts, but it could be worse," he replied.

"So what's the plan now, Boss?" Axel asked Quinn.

Quinn tapped his ear and said nothing for a moment.

"Oh, was that my cue?" Sentry said in Quinn's ear.

"I'm still figuring that out," Quinn replied.

"Ah, gotcha. Well, that was unusual, but not entirely unexpected. And thanks for not telling anyone. As far as rescuing the girl, I still don't have enough information on that. I'm stretching my capabilities from a distance, constrained yet able to bend the rules by adhering strictly to my limitations. So far, I've merged radio frequencies with heat and light waves to form a real-time, albeit rough, surface map. The details blur indoors and underground, though I can discern shapes. Detailed mapping will take longer."

"Why don't we rescue Kira? How's that for a plan?" Jeremy said.

"A little sparse on the details, but I'm in," Axel replied.

"We need to find our doubles. We need more manpower, and we need to map out more of the surroundings before we attempt a rescue," Quinn said.

"You need to move now," Sentry said.

"Where do you think our doubles might be?" Quinn replied.

"Probably looking for us," Dr. Green replied.

"I said move. You've got hostiles closing in," Sentry added.

"We need to leave now," Quinn said before adding, "Which direction?"

"Don't you think we should be looking for Kira first?" Jeremy asked.

"You've got about five seconds before you won't have any more options. Move left and then another left," Sentry said.

"Everyone, run left and then left, now. I don't have time to explain."

Quinn shot out of the room and turned left. The room bustled behind him with the clamor of hard steps and fumbling. Quinn made another left. A few wisps of air and footsteps told him at least one person was close behind.

"Good. Now stay very quiet," Sentry said.

"Someone's coming. Don't make a sound," Quinn whispered.

Quinn gazed around the dimly lit chamber, which he

judged to be around ten by ten meters. He slouched down with his back against the stone wall. The rest of the group was on his left, with the entrance on his right.

A thunderous clapping jolted past the chamber. Loud grunts and snorts accompanied a procession of tremors and vibrations. Quinn then caught a glimmer of a white flash, and then the shaking subsided.

The group remained quiet for another couple of minutes. "How did you know they were coming?" Jeremy asked.

"He can loop time, so obviously he must've seen it in a prior loop," Axel replied.

Quinn remained quiet, analyzing his options and the information Sentry had revealed before he finally spoke. "We need to split up. I'll give you a map of the area. Axel and Jeremy will find our doubles, and Dr. Green and I will find the room that contains a portal with exotic matter. This should allow all of you to relive and remember the loops when they reset, at least until the exotic matter wears off. You'll relive them when you pass through the portal and return, but to remember, I'll need to steal some tech. Once we find what we need, we'll meet here," Quinn said.

"I still have trouble wrapping my head around what it means for us when you die but we keep going," Jeremy said.

"It means we usually die too," Axel said.

"I know that much. I'm just glad we're the lucky version that happens to be along for the ride," Jeremy replied.

"You won't be saying that if Quinn dies again before we can pass through the portal, as this version of you will be dead," Axel added.

"All the more reason to make sure we succeed," Quinn said. He let a few seconds of silence pass and then added, "I might have a way of finding what we need, but we need to hurry," he said.

Quinn sketched out the modified layout on a sheet of paper based on what he'd learned from the prior loops and handed it to Jeremy. "I suspect you might find them somewhere along this route," he said, tracing his finger over a series of pathways on the sketch. "Find them and bring them here," Quinn said.

CHAPTER 19

PLANET SURFACE, EARTH 2/MULTIVERSE 732, LOOP 17

QUINN AND DR. GREEN arrived at the room they'd been searching for. The chamber resembled all the other chambers they'd entered before, except for a small wooden door in the center, barely large enough for them to enter.

"Should we open it?" Quinn asked.

"I can't get a reading on what's on the other side," Sentry told Quinn.

"There's only one way to know," Dr. Green replied.

Quinn cracked open the door, only revealing darkness from the small sliver. He pushed it wider, unfolding only a few hints of dark gray. Finally, he sprung it wide and peered deep inside. He moved his foot as if to take a step.

"Wait," Dr. Green said, holding Quinn by his arm. "Let me go first."

"I get a do-over. You don't."

"That's why you should let me in first," Dr. Green said.

Quinn considered it. If the door was the portal entryway, it made sense to let Dr. Green through first. He'd get a dose of exotic matter in some unknown configuration that would let him relive the time loop even if he didn't remember it. The working theory was that it would forge a nexus and birth an alternate multiverse.

"You're right. You have the honors."

Dr. Green crossed over the boundary and turned to face Quinn. "Well, that was disappointing."

He stepped forward to exit, but something stopped him from returning, like a bird striking a clear windowpane along with a thud. He pounded it with his fist. "I can't cross back."

"Then let's do this together."

Before Dr. Green could protest, Quinn crossed halfway and changed his mind but grabbed Dr. Green's arm and attempted to pull him out. Dr. Green banged against the barrier, but Quinn returned with no problem.

"I had to try it," Quinn said.

"Don't come over just yet. I'll see if I can find anything inside before you do."

"You may get lost. I don't want you stuck there forever," Quinn replied.

Dr. Green turned around. "I have an idea." He pulled out a string and tied it around a quarter, leaving a lot of slack. "I'll use this to retrace my steps. Just give me a couple of minutes," he added.

"Fine. Just be careful," Quinn said.

Dr. Green retreated, releasing more of the string, and backpedaled as each section dropped to the floor. Soon, Dr. Green vanished into the shadows in front of Quinn.

Quinn eyed the quarter for each minute movement. "Can you hear me?"

"Yeah, I can, but I don't see anything else other than this shroud of darkness."

Dr. Green went silent. "You still there?"

He waited a few seconds. "Dr. Green?"

"I feel something. Hold on."

Quinn waited. His heart rate increased. A few taps and clicks echoed through the barrier, and then Dr. Green stepped forward into the dim light.

"There's equipment with a computer server and some controls."

Quinn stepped through the doorway until he was across the threshold.

"You shouldn't have done that."

Quinn receded and thrust his arm forward. It struck an invisible barrier. He stepped forward to the door but hit the barrier again.

"This was the original plan, so don't sweat it."

Quinn turned on his flashlight in the shroud of darkness.

Several corridors down, Axel and Jeremy arrived just ahead of the chamber Quinn outlined on the map.

"I think I hear something," Jeremy said.

Axel crept closer to the entrance, careful not to make a sound. He dropped down toward the floor and peered inside, then jerked his head away from sight. "She's there," he mouthed.

Axel withdrew, and Jeremy glanced inside. Kira sat on the hard ground with her arms bound behind her back. Two guards stood a few meters away, mumbling something he couldn't understand.

Axel motioned his hand to his pistol and whispered, "On three."

Jeremy's eyes widened.

Axel held up his fingers. "One, two, three."

Axel rotated into the entrance and shot at both guards, striking one, who fell and hit his head on a large pedestal. The other ducked and moved to the side. Axel entered and strode left, continuing to fire.

Jeremy followed suit, moving right and firing from the other side. Jeremy struck the edge of his right arm, but not enough to injure him severely. The three of them continued the dance. Axel grazed him from the left, and Jeremy fired another glancing blow, this time on his right leg.

In the middle, Kira shifted, attempting to get the gag out of her mouth. A second later, Jeremy scored a clean hit square in the guard's chest. If he hadn't been wearing armor, he'd be dead. Still, the gear didn't completely protect the guard, and he retreated, stunned. Axel seized the chance and landed a clean shot in the throat.

The guard collapsed on the floor. Jeremy ran over to the two guards' positions and fired several bolts into both limp bodies. A calmness flooded through him but vanished as quickly as it came, replaced by tightness in his chest.

Kira's squirming stopped. She simply stared at Jeremy with uncertain eyes. He hurried over to her and removed the gag, then tore off the bindings around her wrists.

"Thank you."

It took Jeremy a few seconds to speak. "We're planning to meet with our friends. Are they holding any more of your people?"

Axel's brows furrowed.

"They didn't take anyone before they took me, so I can't be sure. But usually, they just kill my people. They want information from me. That's the only reason I'm still alive."

"I'm sorry for what these men have done, but I'm glad they didn't hurt you," Jeremy replied.

Something in her eyes spoke to him, perhaps the pain she must've endured and the strength she needed to overcome it. He wondered how much Quinn might want him to share about their plans and how much she could be trusted.

"I want to come with you."

Axel squinted. "You think Boss would like that?"

"Quinn would want all the help he can get," Jeremy said.

Axel didn't object, but his body language suggested he wasn't completely sold on the idea.

Kira rubbed her wrists. "They'll return soon. We should leave."

"This way," Jeremy said. Kira followed close behind, and Axel took up the rear, glancing in all directions once they left the chamber.

In another corridor, Quinn withdrew another meter from the door, and a metal cube with dials and knobs appeared. It reminded him of something one might read in a steampunk novel. "Jesus. I wonder how many time loops I'll need to figure out this thing."

"Hopefully none. Look at this dial here," Dr. Green said.

Quinn squinted, reading the metered lines etched on the outside glass next to the dial. Small cuneiform characters matched each notch on the vertical scale.

"I recognize these images. We've found it. This has to be the contraption used to safely add exotic matter to each person."

"The tech doesn't exactly inspire confidence."

"This is only the external interface. The actual tech is hidden somewhere between the walls."

Dr. Green studied the stack, carefully reviewing each character along all the vertical and horizontal dials. Quinn turned his focus to the walls that held them, searching for any possible hint of a way out.

After a few minutes, Quinn grew disinterested in their surroundings and joined Dr. Green in studying the control stack.

"I think I'm beginning to understand this," Dr. Green said, and then he spent the next few minutes discussing the fine details of how he suspected the controls worked.

Quinn restated Dr. Green's assumptions a couple of times until he was semi-confident that he grasped the basic theoretical workings of what the device did. He'd need to study the specifics later.

Quinn's ear crackled. "My data suggests there's an 87 percent probability Dr. Green is correct. And there's a 99 percent probability activating the machine is your only way out," Sentry said.

CHAPTER 20

Tier 1, Earth 2/Multiverse 732, simulator, loop 17

CAMERON SAT ON the bench in the simulator. This time, Sentry changed the setting to her old high school lunchroom. One of the female work staff stood behind the clear panels covering the food. Aside from her, they were alone.

The room was just as Cameron remembered, stirring memories of Quinn, Jeremy, and their old crew. She often pondered the experiences from Quinn's former life that she'd missed, feeling a twinge of guilt for longing for a past she hadn't been part of, despite Quinn's world-saving deeds. The simulator offered an unexpected chance to experience that history, not by returning to her past self but closely enough.

Cameron took a fork and dug into the only menu item she really liked, lightly salted tater tots. "There's got to be something else we can do for them," Cameron told Sentry.

"I'm helping Quinn as much as I can, but if we take any direct action from here, we'll likely die in a matter of seconds. I have made great strides in communicating with Quinn and observing the surface despite the constraints from the construct, but there are still limitations."

"I still don't get why you don't want Quinn to let his team know about your communication. If we do have someone working against us, he'll figure it out in another loop."

"That won't do any good for this version of you. And even if you did manage to survive, there's always the possibility that a spy would be playing the long game. We could win this battle only to lose a more important war. I can help you, but you're going to have to trust me," Sentry said.

Cameron remained silent, only placing her hand over her stomach. "If there's one thing I've learned from this unconventional life, it's that humility is underrated. People who say they know everything never do, and people who doubt themselves don't give themselves enough credit. Always assume things could go wrong. So tell me, what happens if they do?"

"There are levels of wrong, but the worst thing would be the destruction of our universe, the entire multiverse, and the totality of all multiverses in existence. Though I don't think that last one is a possibility, more like a cluster of multiverses gets destroyed or corrupted."

"And you think your plan can prevent this from happening?"

"Not in the slightest. What I can do as a sentient AI based on a real person is limited, especially given the constraints of the construct. Quinn and his pals will have to do most of the heavy lifting. But if my assumptions are correct," he said and then let a few seconds pass, "I mean within a 93 percent probability, then you play an equally as important role as Quinn."

"Care to elaborate?"

"Let's just say that things aren't as dire for you as for everyone else if Quinn screws up."

On the planet's surface, Dr. Green turned the dial on the largest knob. The glass dial flared green and crackled. Dr. Green fumbled toward the entrance. "I think this should work. I'll need to go through first, and then you tell me what you see on these two dials."

"You sure about this?"

"Sure as I can be on an alternate planet in a different multiverse with people trying to kill us. But, yeah, it should work."

"I like the way you think," Quinn said.

Dr. Green stepped across the threshold between the entrance and the door. The first half of his body crossed seamlessly, followed by his other half. "So far, so good. Now let's see if this does what's expected."

Quinn inhaled and waited for Dr. Green's instructions. The left dial moved to the right. "One of the dials is moving."

"Perfect. Tell me exactly which character the arrow is closest to."

"It looks like the symbol for the lotus, a small mound on the bottom with a long tube and a lotus on top, dead center."

"Ha! I knew it."

"So what does that mean?"

"Look at the other knob. Tell me exactly where it's pointing."

Quinn went on to describe the glyphs in exacting detail, which included three separate markings in a single cluster.

"You've just dosed me with enough exotic matter for one thousand lives. This control center can measure how much exotic matter I have remaining tethered to this body and mind. If I die, I'll be able to return and retain all my memories. We need to get the rest of the team here."

Quinn thought through numerous possibilities, and then his eyes widened. "Do you think it could accurately measure how much exotic matter I have remaining on me?"

"It should, and I think you'll have to go through the machine anyway to cross back over. The only problem is I'll need to return inside to check the readings, which means I'll need to reenter through the portal. I think it will let me cross again."

Quinn wondered how those using the machine normally ran the controls. A tremor interrupted his thoughts. "Alright. Let's hurry."

Dr. Green hurried into the room and analyzed the readings. "Now your turn."

Quinn took no time stepping through the door. Once he was across, Dr. Green's eyes widened. "You're going to love this."

"What is it?"

"The number of loops you have remaining is off the charts. You didn't get dosed, since I wanted to see how much residual exotic matter you already have, so this is all you. And we suspected your situation was special from your initial loop before the supernova."

"Exactly how many are off the charts?"

"It's only got five digits. Yours is stuck at 99,999. I suspect it's higher, but this essentially means you practically have an infinite number of loops."

"What about the energy required to loop longer time frames like you theorized earlier?"

"The way the cuneiform is written . . ."

Small rocks fell from the ceiling and interrupted Dr. Green's sentence.

"Let's get out of here," Quinn shouted.

Dr. Green ran toward the door. Once he reached the threshold, it shot him back. Several more tremors rocked the corridor and broke more rubble free. Quinn cried out, but a mound of debris drowned out his calls.

Tier 1, Earth 2/Multiverse 732, loop 18

AFTER RE-ENTERING THE singularity, Quinn followed the same path as the prior loop and made his way to the simulation room. He willed his thoughts to the machine and quickly calmed his mind to achieve the lowered brainwave frequency needed to communicate directly with Sentry's avatar.

Quinn's consciousness emerged in the familiar simulation room. He blinked, adjusting quickly. The hum of machinery and a soft blue light bathed the room. Sentry stood before him and said, "You haven't checked yet if Dr. Green remembers the last loop?"

The environment faded. In an instant, the room transformed into a simulation of the planet's surface near the Great Pyramid. Two large reclining chairs sat in the sliver of meager shade. Sentry sipped on a lemonade. "My calculations show we have an 87 percent probability of avoiding the creation of an energy bubble if we pull in Dr. Green now."

"Let's do it."

A third chair appeared next to them. A second later, Dr Green appeared.

"I see you got the message. We have limited time, so to speak. What do you remember?" Sentry asked.

"I remember everything from the last loop."

"Excellent," Sentry said.

Over the next hour in simulated time, Dr. Green and Quinn discussed what they remembered and hashed out a strategy to get the other team members to the doorway.

"Time to head to the surface for real," Quinn said.

CHAPTER 21

EARTH 2/MULTIVERSE 732, PLANET SURFACE, LOOP 18

QUINN SMILED AND looked up. "Right on cue."

A second smaller shuttle approached, lowering to just a few feet from the exact spot as the landing party shuttle. The rest of the group eyed the shuttle until it landed.

"You sure this is going to work, Boss?"

"With Dr. Green now part of the loop, we're one step closer," Quinn replied.

"Don't forget, no one else must know I can communicate with you outside Tier 1. If you copy, say 'Let's do this,'" Sentry said in Quinn's ear.

"Let's do this," Quinn said.

The four of them sprinted across the desert toward the pyramid's right side. Once they covered half the distance, Dr. Green and Jeremy split off toward the left, and Quinn and Axel shifted right.

As they made their way closer to the Great Pyramid, Kira and Ubuntu entered Quinn's visual field well in the distance. Quinn and Axel doubled their gait. Quinn's lungs burned, but he didn't let up. He kept pushing his legs to the limit until a few minutes later they arrived near Ubuntu's party.

"Kira, Ubuntu," Quinn said.

"I take it we've met before," Ubuntu replied.

"Boy, do we have a story to tell," Quinn added.

Dr. Green and Jeremy arrived at the base of the pyramid. Dr. Green skimmed his hand along the grooves near three large limestone bricks. He repeated the task a few seconds more until he stopped. "There you are."

A large section of bricks shifted just enough to create a passage for them to enter. "Ladies first," Dr. Green said.

"Who you calling a lady?" Jeremy paused, "but if you insist."

Jeremy squeezed through the passage, and Dr. Green followed behind him.

"The path is on the left. We'll need to hurry if we're going to make it," Dr. Green said before adding, "This is the strangest feeling I've ever had."

Jeremy had a strange feeling too listening to Dr. Green discuss what he'd been wanting since he was a kid. That desire kicked into overdrive when Quinn returned from the future in Jeremy's past.

"I know what you're thinking."

"What am I thinking?" Jeremy asked.

"You want a do-over."

Jeremy didn't say anything. He just kept following Dr. Green through the corridors.

"You'll need to be careful on this next turn. If you hit the pedestal, we'll be swarmed by scarabs in seconds, so hang as far right as you can once we enter the chamber."

Dr. Green entered first. Jeremy slowed his pace and moved to the right once he squeezed through, watching his movements until the platform appeared.

"There's a smaller one toward the right, just a few feet after the main pedestal, so as soon as you reach the end, start moving left but not too far left, so you don't nick the base from behind as you squeeze through."

A gust of wind blew through the passageway. Jeremy tensed, and he froze mid-stride. For a moment, Jeremy thought he'd failed and the scarabs would soon pour in, but after a few seconds, the wind abated and the tightness in his chest relaxed.

He continued inching forward until they trudged past the smaller pedestal. Once they reached the next corridor, the passageway opened. "It's just up ahead," Dr. Green said.

"Of course I want a do-over. How far back can I go?"

"Uncertain, but once we leave, you'll likely only reach the singularity's entrance. After returning home, you can probably only return to the moment of re-entry. So, you won't be able to revisit your childhood or undo awkward moments."

"What makes you think I have any awkward moments?"

Dr. Green laughed. "Isn't that what you 'normals' talk about all the time?"

Jeremy had to think for a moment. He'd nearly forgotten about Dr. Green's autism. Dr. Green's daily routine practices helped him almost master the art of deceiving most people at first glance, and Jeremy was constantly preoccupied with Quinn saving the world.

"Touché."

"That's an awfully big word."

"Not so much."

Footsteps interrupted their banter.

"This way," Dr. Green whispered.

Jeremy followed Dr. Green left. The corridor soon opened into a dark room. Dr. Green stepped forward and disappeared from view. "Step forward," Dr. Green said, still invisible.

Jeremy moved ahead into the shroud of darkness and joined Dr. Green, now visible. "The device is right in front of us. Once you enter, you won't be able to leave until you've finished. We think it's a failsafe mechanism."

Jeremy breezed across. "You don't have to convince me."

"Stand over there and hold this."

Dr. Green handed Jeremy a small sphere attached to a skinny tube that fed through a larger box covered in knobs and dials.

"It won't hurt. I promise—" Dr. Green paused and then added, "mostly."

Jeremy's eyes widened, and then a few sparks flew from the sphere into his hand, flowing up through and over his body. A bubble of shimmering light enveloped him. A second later, the bubble faded.

"Let's see if this thing works. Walk through the door and wait there."

Jeremy let go of the sphere and returned across the entrance. A moment later, Dr. Green joined him. "You've got a full charge. Now it's time to find our doubles."

Dr. Green tapped the microsphere to prime the device to measure his exotic matter output but knew he would be unable to read it once he passed through the threshold.

Outside the Great Pyramid, Quinn and Axel hustled several hundred yards toward the smaller pyramids and then came to a complete stop.

"Here," Quinn said.

Axel swept his forearm across the ground, unveiling a smooth stone face beneath the sand.

CHAPTER 22

Earth 2/Multiverse, planet surface, loop 18

DR. GREEN SLOUCHED DOWN to the ground, careful to avoid the maze of pedestals and obstructions strewn across the long, dark corridor. Jeremy took up the rear.

"The underground entrance should be just up ahead."

Jeremy focused on his movements. "What I still don't understand is . . . Hold on. I see something."

The scuttle of swarming insects echoed in front of them. Before they had time to react, scarab beetles surrounded them, crawling over every inch of their bodies. Jeremy jumped up, flinging them wildly off his person. A few crawled into his mouth, and he coughed them out.

"Scarabs are harm—" Dr. Green said, but the swarm cut him off. He fell over, screaming. "Something's wrong," he said.

Jeremy shook himself, jumping up and down. "They must be modified like the animals Quinn told us about in the prior loop."

He fired his laser pistol and lit up the room. More scarabs

poured in from a single hole in the sidewall. "Fire there," Jeremy said.

They aimed their pistols and shot in a nearly continuous burst. Scarab corpses piled into heaps until the scuttling stopped. Jeremy kept firing. Dr. Green forced Jeremy's arm down.

"Don't waste the charges. These aren't unlimited, and we'll need them for later."

Jeremy's hands trembled. He stood frozen, his eyes shifting left and right.

"We've got to keep moving. Follow me."

Dr. Green plucked one of the insects and placed it in his pocket, then swatted the insect mound out of his way and stepped forward. "Stay close."

A few times, Dr. Green turned, and Jeremy was well behind, motionless. Each time, Dr. Green called his name and urged him forward, and Jeremy eventually caught up to speed.

"If I'm right, my guess is our doubles will be in one of the three upcoming corridors," Dr. Green said, stepping forward.

"Not bad, not bad," Dr. Green's carbon copy said, waiting a moment before adding, "Still, it took you long enough."

Jeremy's eyes widened. He stared at both versions of Dr. Green, both wearing unique outfits. The dim lighting made it difficult to discern minute variations, but each copy's hair was different enough in style and color for Jeremy to distinguish them. Dr. Green's alternate self wore a 1920s-style baseball cap that clashed with the rest of his outfit. He was also a few pounds lighter and with a few more gray hairs.

Jeremy then caught a glimpse of himself, one he almost envied. Something about his face made his appearance more certain. His clothes were more beaten up, but underneath the recent wear was more stylish garb than he would normally wear.

"I see you met up with our friends," Jeremy's double said.

"Friends?" the original Jeremy replied.

"The scarabs. We're using them as an early warning system in case the others found their way here before you guys arrived. Speaking of you guys, what happened to the rest of you?"

Jeremy opened his mouth to speak but then stopped himself. "How do we know which version of us we're speaking to?"

"Did you modify them too?" Dr. Green asked.

"Don't blame us. I'm sure we have The Way to thank for that," his alternate self replied.

"Quinn thinks we should bring you with us since you don't have a ride home. It was you who sent us the video on the array, *wasn't it*?" Jeremy asked.

Someone else in the darkness approached from behind, and then another. A hooded figure slid in from behind and then took the front.

"You bet your ass it was us," Gary said, wearing an EverQuest IV black T-shirt and hover shoes.

Jeremy's eyes lit up. "Gary!"

"Glad to see you, too, old friend. And there's more of us home if we can just hitch a ride."

Another figure emerged from behind Gary.

Gary hovered a few inches off the ground. The hover shoes were silent, and Gary was stable at rest.

"Love the new kicks," Jeremy said.

"I hate to break up this little reunion, but where are the rest of you?" Quinn's copy said.

"My Quinn and our friend Axel went looking for you guys, but he had another stop to make before then. In case we met up with you first, he gave us some instructions for you," Jeremy said.

He handed Quinn a small piece of paper, which alternate Quinn promptly read. Alternate Quinn's face contorted. "Getting off this version of Earth isn't the only reason we called you. There's something else happening on this planet."

The floor vibrated. On the far end of the chamber, a corner of the ground inched higher and released a torrent of scorpions toward the adjacent entrance. Gary rotated toward the disturbance. Alternate Quinn and Dr. Green turned and grabbed their pistols. Jeremy and Dr. Green followed suit.

"More friends?" Jeremy said.

The march of steps echoed into the chamber. "That's our cue to leave. Follow me," Gary said.

Gary glided quickly down the corridor where Dr. Green and Jeremy arrived and then hung a left. Dr. Green struggled to keep pace with the rest of them, but alternate Quinn tossed a smoke bomb the size of a plumb behind Dr. Green, obscuring the view behind them.

The process repeated a few times down several corridors. Finally, they reached a large chamber. Once they were all inside, Gary struck a large stone that was chest level near the entrance. The wall moved behind them. A few seconds later, it closed completely, sealing them in.

Jeremy turned back at the people staring at him. A large group of what he assumed were residents sat behind him. Most were preoccupied with mundane things, but a few stood and watched them intently.

Axel and Quinn emerged from behind them. "Good, you're all here," Quinn said.

Quinn stepped forward as did alternate Quinn, both now facing each other. "We've got a lot to talk about," alternate Quinn said.

CHAPTER 23

EARTH 2/MULTIVERSE 732, PLANET SURFACE, LOOP 18

ALTERNATE QUINN AND his team stood facing Quinn and his ground crew. "We're not that different, you and I. Our timelines diverged when the array was under attack. Saboteurs attempted to commandeer the entire array. I decided to separate the array into sections and move out of Earth's orbit to avoid a collision."

Quinn listened. Jeremy and Axel inspected Quinn's expressions, but he gave no hint of what he was thinking.

"I'm listening to all of it," Sentry said in Quinn's ear.

"The funny thing is, I don't remember it until after it happened. For some reason, I was catapulted into the 1980s. And even stranger, I was thrown into my father's body."

Quinn's eyes widened. "Do you remember any of this?" alternate Quinn asked.

"Nope. Not a thing. For us, Tier 1 was shot through a singularity into an alternate Earth with modified dinosaurs. The planet had a different array, and something guarding it.

We barely got out of it alive. But we did learn something valuable," Quinn said.

"Into his father's body? That is interesting. Hold on, Quinn. Let me check a few things," Sentry said.

Over the next ten minutes, alternate Quinn filled in Quinn and his team on the time he'd spent in the 1980s with his mother and how someone killed her in that timeline, how he teamed up with Dr. Green and discovered the spheres with Scott Channing's father, and how everything was all connected.

With every bit of new information, Sentry updated his systems and recalculated probabilities and what he thought The Way was planning. "This is amazing if true. I'm not sure what to make of some of it. Give me a moment," Sentry whispered.

Alternate Quinn stopped speaking, and everyone else remained speechless for what Quinn felt was longer than it was. Quinn broke the silence. "We found the same video cache. Or maybe not the same video cache, but something almost exactly the same. But I never had the opportunity to travel to the future, or a version of it," Quinn said.

"That's part of the reason I'm here. At the moment of our divergence, the timeline created two separate halves of our possible existence. From what I've seen, most of those versions who went to the future have fought hard to stop The Way," alternate Quinn said.

Axel interrupted, "Is this where you say the rest who didn't turn out to be the bad guys?"

"Not all, just a higher percentage. Most end up doing nothing or mentally looping in time and reliving their lives, ignoring their present. But something more sinister is happening."

Dust shook from the ceiling and blinded Quinn. His eyes burned. A continuous bang rattled the walls, filling the room with a brown cloud of dust. Those around him buried their faces in their arms.

Alternate Quinn coughed. "They've found us. We have to get out of here."

Those in the room lost their balance. Quinn attempted to steady himself but fell to the floor. A crack opened on the right wall and blinded Quinn for a few moments until his eyes adjusted.

"Quinn, I know what you need to do," Sentry said.

Quinn blinked his eyes, barely able to see. "What's that?" he said.

"You need to die before anyone else. Unfortunately, that means that only Dr. Green will remember anything from prior loops, and he won't remember anything from this last loop. What I've calculated is that in the new timeline, only those with the prior ability during the current loop will retain that ability. That means you and Dr. Green. Jeremy will still need to go through the machine again and so will Axel, who's never been," Sentry replied.

The hole grew larger. Two large animals appeared, one with a large neck that was heading in for a pounce against the sandstone wall.

"I thought everyone who went through the machine would retain information from the loop," Quinn said.

"They will, for just that version of themselves. The only way that more than one will retain that information is if they die at the same time. Otherwise, when you arrive in the singularity, only those who died with you in a prior loop will retain any information, and just from the point in which you all died together. So that means not everyone will remember every loop," Sentry added.

"A muddled mess," Quinn replied.

Another beast emerged behind the first one, slightly smaller and just small enough to bolt through the large hole he had created. "Run!" Jeremy said.

"What if we all die together? Does it have to be at the same second?" Quinn asked.

Jeremy squinted at Quinn during the chatter.

"Not exactly the same second. Some physics parameters determine the exact moment, but I calculate an 88 percent probability of success if it occurs within the same fifteen seconds," Sentry said.

Quinn needed time to think, but giant beasts and falling bricks made that nearly impossible. "Dr. Green and Jeremy, listen closely. Everyone else, aim your pistols at the creatures and keep running."

Alternate Quinn squinted like he suspected he knew what Quinn was about to do but didn't know why. Most of the group fired their weapons. Quinn, Dr. Green, and Jeremy hesitated, struggling to stay upright as they dodged falling debris.

"We don't have much time, but you're going to have to trust me on this. For us to all remember this and future loops, we need to die within a few seconds of each other at most. You know I don't like the idea of suicide, even for the purposes of a do-over, but it's the only way to bring us all in together," Quinn said.

"I don't mind waiting for the next one," Jeremy said.

"For us, it means we'd need to get you to the portal room. This version of you would be in a different timeline. Our holographic minds won't be tethered to the same one. And we don't have that much time. On three, we aim our pistols at our heads and fire. Our minds will be thrown to the entry of the singularity, but the final decision is up to you. On three," Quinn said.

CHAPTER 24

Tier 1, Earth 2/Multiverse 732, loop 19

THE MOMENT THE screen displayed "Tier 1 entering singularity," Quinn replayed what he could in his mind. He wanted to rush off to speak with Jeremy and Dr. Green, but he didn't want to risk activating the energy field, as he still wasn't certain what action triggered it.

Upon securing the timeline, Quinn summoned Cameron, Dr. Green, Jeremy, and Axel to the simulation room and instructed them to wait while he connected to the terminal first.

Quinn followed the breathing exercises needed to change his brainwave state, which he'd gotten better at in the prior loops, and connected with Sentry.

The simulation created a vast open field with two concrete benches in the center. Sentry sat facing Quinn on the opposing bench. "So you've been able to scan my thoughts. Any ideas?"

Sentry smiled. "Fascinating. So I reached out to you

beyond the construct, wonderful. I'm making those adjustments to my system now."

"Why didn't you want me to let anyone else know you were able to contact me?"

Sentry smiled. "That's as much of a mystery to me as it is to you. I haven't run the calculations, and I'm not sure what I uncovered in the prior timeline. But from what you've learned in the current one, your suspicions are well founded."

"You think we have a snitch?" Quinn asked.

"Maybe not like what happened on your prior mission, but it makes sense that The Way has surveillance devices set up on the surface. Those who can remember their loops will use the information for future ones, just like you would."

Quinn sat silently.

"I can read your general thoughts, you know. And I can tell you're still not satisfied."

"True," Quinn said. The ambient light flickered. "But what I'm more interested in is if we can get any closer to destroying that beacon. If we don't, no amount of time looping is going to get us home. Even if we manage to stop The Way from whatever it is they're doing here, we could be stuck," he added.

After Quinn spoke those words, Dr. Green, Jeremy, and Axel appeared sitting on benches next to him.

"I was thinking the same thing, Boss. And when do I get to join in on all the fun?" Axel asked.

"Now that I've been brought in on the loop, I'm sure it will be in no time at all," Jeremy said.

"Pay attention," Sentry said.

The meadow vanished, replaced with desert and pyramids as they appeared on the alternate planet. "You'll need to follow my instructions down to the letter. I've been able to add in the information from all of you the best I can, and this is what I've come up with."

The simulation shifted, moving them through each corridor they'd be traversing once they arrived on the planet. It had them focus on getting Axel through the looping portal first and then self-immolate for a repeat loop later, at which point they'd meet up with the alternate Quinn and his team.

"I don't like the idea of killing myself, even if I loop again later," Axel said.

Quinn listened, remembering what Axel had told him about his family. "I know this is tough, especially for you, but you will have a continuity of consciousness." He paused and then added, "Having more people on our side will help us stop them for good."

"Won't they just keep returning in different versions, in different universes and multiverses?"

"I can't say much of anything with *100 percent* certainty, but this is the multiverse that they're using to collapse others. This is the one that's been impacting our multiverse. And they are subject to the same rules of physics we are. They just know them better. But if we stop this now, it could be permanent, at least for us. That's the best I can do," Quinn said.

"Shouldn't we try to help our duplicates do the same thing? And what about Cameron and the rest of our crew? I'd hate to be her in the world where you just died," Jeremy said.

"Don't be an ass. We've all got a job to do," Axel said.

"I'm sorry. I just . . ."

Quinn cut him off. "This right here is what matters. If what our doubles said is true, we have to stop the convergence, and this is where it starts. Halting it at the source ends it."

"Will that stop them for good?"

"I don't know about for good, but it should be good enough, at least for now. I may be able to loop time, but I'm not a god. No one is. It takes tremendous effort and coordination to do something on this scale. Whatever remains of The Way might continue their effort, but to what end?" Quinn replied.

Jeremy turned his attention to Sentry. "What do you think?"

"My math predicts an 88 percent probability that if you stop The Way here, they won't be able to resurface within your lifetime. And there's only a 43 percent chance they'll resurface again at all."

"And how exactly did you make those calculations?" Jeremy asked.

"I have the construct, and I have the information from all your experiences. At least mostly, low res. But it's good enough."

"How much of our lives can you see from our heads?" Axel said.

"Only what you want me to see, but that's good enough to find enough data points and variable approximations to plot a path."

"I'm not too picky. I'm looking forward to joining the loop so I can execute some of those Way scum with impunity. Mind you, I do that already. It would just be nice to know I could let loose on those mofos," Axel said.

"Don't get too trigger-happy. We want to get as much intel from them as we can before we leave this place," Quinn added.

"Don't worry. I'm *really* good at getting intel."

Quinn fought back a smile. He couldn't help but imagine

one of the bad guys screaming like a little girl at the hands of Axel. For a moment, he had almost forgotten what had happened to Axel's sister. "We'll have to accept those odds for the moment. Now let's get going. We don't waste this loop if we don't have to. Priority one is to get Axel to the portal. We stick together, so we reset the loop if and when we need to. Once Axel is through, we'll gather what intel we can and reset before the end of the day or when we're found out, whichever is first."

"What do you think, Sentry?" Axel asked.

Sentry smiled. "Thanks for treating me like a human."

"Well you are or at least were, so it's not like we're talking to a machine. You just happen to be connected to one."

"That's true, though I am still missing some of my memories. As far as the answer to your question, Quinn is right. The priority is to get you all on the same loop, which means getting you through the portal and resetting at your earliest convenience to avoid wasting the opportunity."

The simulation shifted. The walls displayed the exact locations of the corridors each of them remembered in all the prior loops and merged the data into one. On a second wall, the simulation unveiled an interior image of the corridor next to the location.

"Now this is what I'm talkin' about," Axel said.

Once they memorized the layout, Sentry ran a simulation dozens of times. In each instance, Sentry added something unexpected. The team gained speed, albeit unevenly, with each iteration. Sentry pushed the reverse time dilation to its limits until they had succeeded dozens of times in different scenarios, ranging from nothing unexpected to the worst possible luck they could imagine.

Quinn and his team exited the simulation and followed the prior loop in exacting detail until they landed at the surface. A few moments later, the second micro shuttle holding the spheres landed separately.

Sentry whispered a slew of instructions that only Quinn could hear, supplemental details that would've been too difficult to explain without revealing Sentry's new capabilities, and then he added, "And once you've got Axel through the loop portal, he'll be immune to frozen time once you activate the spheres if and when you need to activate them. Just make sure you're close enough to the device so the whole thing doesn't go kablooey."

Quinn opened the micro-shuttle and placed two spheres in his satchel, then gave one each to Dr. Green and Jeremy.

"Alright, let's do this," Quinn said.

The team made a beeline for the Great Pyramid. One hundred meters into the run, the sky darkened, not a lot but just enough that most people would notice. Quinn glanced up. "What the hell is that?"

The team slowed their stride and eventually came to a halt, each member looking up. The slow light change reminded Quinn of an eclipse, only the sun was not obstructed. It was as if the night sky were bleeding into one half of the horizon, with the sun and the day on the other half. Stars appeared where they shouldn't be visible.

"I hope this isn't what I think it is," Dr. Green said.

"They must be almost finished," Sentry told Quinn.

"We've still got time. Stick with the plan, and keep moving," Quinn said.

"You got it, Boss." Axel moved first and led the rest of the team forward.

"He's just showing off," Jeremy said.

Quinn's brows furrowed. "No. He wants to get to the loop portal."

Quinn and the team continued their brisk pace toward the Great Pyramid, their eyes fixed on the bizarre sky above. As they moved forward, the celestial anomaly intensified, spreading like an inkblot, slowly engulfing the entire expanse. The stars shone, their light on the surface washed out by the sun's light from the opposite side of the sky.

"Are you sure we have time? This doesn't look great," Jeremy said.

"Just put one foot in front of the other," Axel replied.

Quinn's heart skipped a beat. For a moment, his peripheral vision faded into darkness, and he breathed erratically. The ringing in his ears drowned out most of the surrounding noise.

Axel picked up the pace into a military rhythm. Everyone struggled to keep up. Dr. Green was farthest behind. He soon caught up but then fell behind again. The sprint reminded him of the video they'd seen. It wasn't the same, but Quinn sensed the same emotion his double must have felt in that moment.

They reached the entrance of the Great Pyramid, the massive stone structure looming before them. Quinn stole a glance up. It hadn't changed. The mental pressure eased, but just a smidge.

The dimly lit corridor stretched out ahead, leading them deeper into the heart of the pyramid. Axel took the lead. The rest of the team followed closely. Their eyes scanned the surroundings for any signs of danger.

As they made their way through the labyrinthine corridors, they returned to one of the first sections Quinn recalled with a hybrid of Egyptian and ancient, almost alien, symbols etched into the walls. From what Dr. Green and Quinn had deciphered in past loops, the hieroglyphics depicted worlds converging, a merging of timelines, and the presence of a powerful entity at the center.

Sentry used his new abilities to scan the area with modified radio waves that bounced off the area. He ran near-instantaneous calculations.

"From what I'm seeing, you were correct in your assumptions. This is a nexus point. They're using this planet, this universe, to collide worlds. I can't explain the science behind it, though I could speculate, but the effects are clear enough. They've set up a series of portals to funnel exotic matter, both to and from different multiverses."

Quinn reflected on Sentry's words. He still didn't fully understand how that was possible and wondered how the past and the nature of time might play into all of it.

Finally, they reached the chamber that housed the entrance. At its center stood the time loop portal, a fog of darkness at its opening.

Axel stepped forward. Quinn, Dr. Green, and Jeremy stood beside him, their pistols gripped tightly in their hands. They exchanged looks that communicated Axel's readiness to step across.

"After we confirm Axel's exotic matter level and exit the portal, we fire on my count simultaneously. Our minds will be thrown to the entry of the singularity. Ready?" Quinn said.

The team fixed their eyes on the portal before them. Quinn counted down. "One . . . two . . . three!"

In perfect harmony, the team aimed their laser pistols at their heads and fired. Gunshots echoed through the chamber, followed by a blinding flash of light.

CHAPTER 25

Tier 1, Earth 2/Multiverse 732, loop 20

QUINN INHALED. HE hated the way he returned but was happy he did. His body tensed. The screen displayed "Tier 1 entering singularity," and Quinn replayed what he could in his mind. He wanted to rush off to speak with Jeremy and Dr. Green, but he didn't want to risk activating the energy field, still uncertain what action triggered it.

Quinn smiled at Cameron, and he wondered how much of the past twenty loops she read on his face and how it would impact their future and their future child. He didn't like keeping anything from her, and each time the loop repeated, he wanted to give her a play-by-play. He cared the most but knew the least about what was going on. He hated that more than needing to repeat the loop.

Quinn eyed the time and sent a message for Cameron, Dr. Green, Jeremy, and Axel to meet him in the simulation room. Quinn told the others to wait to use the terminal while he connected first.

Quinn followed the breathing exercises needed to change his brainwaves and connected with Sentry.

"We did it. We were able to bring Axel in, but weren't able to find the other team."

Quinn and Sentry sat alone. Sentry deciphered Quinn's thoughts and reconstructed his actions from the previous nineteen loops as much as possible.

"Interesting. Give me a moment, and I'll run some more calculations."

Quinn let his thoughts fade into the background and took in the surroundings. The environment morphed slowly with the passing seconds. Birds chirped in the background, but a subtle change in chirping alerted Quinn to the updates. It was more than the last loop. Sentry sensed Quinn's mental state and frustrations and synced the room to have a calming effect.

Two more benches materialized, with Quinn's team appearing on them moments later.

"So did it work?"

"Damn straight it worked, Boss."

Quinn smiled. "Welcome to the team."

"I thought I was already a member of the team."

"You're late to the party," Jeremy added.

The simulation surroundings shifted. The chirping birds quieted. The greenery faded into brown. The benches remained, but they now sat in the Great Pyramid's shadow.

"Do you remember this from last time?" Sentry asked.

"I've got mad skills, bro," Axel replied.

"You'll need more. Now that you're in the loop." He paused. "See what I did there?"

"Yeah, we got it," Jeremy replied.

"As I was saying, pun intended, you have a new objective. You have two, actually, but the primary is to find your alternate selves once again. Now that you're all in the loop, you can work on the distributed defensive strategy. I'll integrate that into the training, and Quinn will go over the details on how you'll work with your duplicates once you get on the planet."

"This will be a breeze," Axel said.

Sand shot into the air. Everyone except for Sentry squinted their eyes. "I wouldn't be so sure about that," Quinn said.

Quinn jostled a few inches to the right, and the others shook as well.

"What is that?" Jeremy asked.

"What you might be up against," Sentry replied.

A loud stomping echoed from behind them and grew louder. Quinn turned. In some distance he couldn't make out, several large creatures towered over the desert sand and raced toward them.

The creatures' skin resembled the cracked desert earth and had a shade that transitioned between dark mahogany and rust, making them initially blend in with the barren landscape. Each stood on four massive, pillar-like legs. Their thunderous footfalls created mini-sandstorms with every step.

"With a new objective, you'll need a new set of obstacles," Sentry said, smiling.

"We'll lick these bastards just like we did in the last training," Axel said.

Dr. Green turned and faced one of the oversized beasts thundering his way. His eyes widened. Thick scales covered its skin, and slime pooled down from its giant teeth. Upon their broad backs, thick spikes jutted out, almost like the serrated edge of an ancient blade. The spikes, though appearing solid, swayed as they moved, producing a soft chime.

"I'm not licking any of those creatures," Dr. Green replied.

"That's not what he meant," Jeremy added.

"I know what he meant. But in both senses of the word, it ain't happening."

"Don't worry, we'll find a way to get them to do it themselves, and please get along, will you?" Quinn said.

Jeremy frowned.

"That I gotta see," Axel added.

"Get a crackin'," Sentry said, and then he vanished from the simulation.

Three more beasts appeared in front of them, materializing out of thin air. Their faces, if they could be called that, were a nightmarish mosaic of ancient carvings, resembling Egyptian hieroglyphs. Two sunken eyes, deep pools of black, shimmered with a moist sheen. There was no discernible nose, but a gaping maw opened, revealing multiple rows of sharp, jagged teeth, each the size of a human hand. From this mouth, they emitted a frightening low growl.

The beasts converged on the four of them. As they drew closer, they radiated intense heat like the searing breath of a forge with hints of sulfur and charred stone. The closest creature swung its thick tail toward them. Axel bent backward, his knees forming a forty-five-degree angle as the tip of its tail sliced the edge of Axel's cheek.

"You'll pay for that," Axel said. He snatched two laser pistols from his side and fired the left and right in quick succession.

"Aim for the eyes," Dr. Green said.

"I'm aiming for something a little more sensitive," Axel said and dropped his stance, shooting into the edge of the animal's trunk. "But feel free to blind the bastard while I hit it where it counts."

Four more creatures appeared in a line behind the first and soon surrounded them in a circle.

"We need to put our backs together and spin in a circle," Axel said.

Quinn sensed a change in Axel. "This isn't going to work," he said. He worried Axel joining the loop might've taken some of the fight out of him. The prior time around, Axel was more meticulous and aggressive, but he watched his approach as if his life depended on it, even during the simulation training. Now, something was off.

Axel's movements became more erratic, his shots less accurate. Quinn's concern grew as Axel struggled to fend off the encroaching creatures. Dr. Green and Jeremy fired nonstop into the beasts bearing down on them, but they were outnumbered and overwhelmed.

"We need to confuse them. Run toward them, and then we'll split in opposite directions just before we collide. And, Axel, now's not the time to get cocky," Quinn said.

A burst of wind destabilized Quinn. A second gust alerted him to the large animal's arrival. Quinn spun around, but the force of the air shoved him to the ground. He struggled to push himself up. The dark bottom of a large foot grew larger as its looming surface came closer to smashing Quinn's head.

The creatures lunged forward, but Axel's shots found their mark, striking the creatures' vulnerable spots. Dr. Green and Jeremy unleashed a barrage of laser fire, forcing the creature to divert its attention. Quinn pushed himself up and shot several rounds into the creature's neck.

The animal staggered, and then its right knee went down. The force of its weight toppled the creature onto its left side.

They focused their fire on the downed beast. Once the creature was dead, they maneuvered into a defensive position using the corpse as a staging area. One by one, they picked off the animals, charging them. With each defeated creature, the team's confidence grew, and Quinn stepped in to temper their enthusiasm. They worked in unison until their movements paired. Finally, the last creature succumbed to their combined assault. The place became silent, but laser smoke and the aroma of burnt flesh hung in the air.

The simulation shifted once more, and the team found themselves standing in the vast open field they had encountered at the beginning. This time, twice as many creatures appeared and twice the size.

"Come on, Boss. There's no way they can be this big," Axel said.

"Prepare for the unexpected," Quinn said.

A second later, a tall, robed man climbed out from underneath a hidden opening five steps in front of them and slashed at Dr. Green with a razor-sharp katana and then plunged it into his heart. He fell to the floor.

"Reset," Axel said.

"Delay that," Quinn added.

"You want us to play this simulation out until the end? I thought you said if we die at different times, we don't sync up with that version of us," Axel said.

"Some of us will, and we need to hone our skills. We're all in the loop now. Even if we don't retain all the memories as a group, collectively we have more knowledge with each iteration," Quinn replied.

"You mean just the four of us on the surface. The rest of our crew aren't in the loop," Jeremy added.

"There's nothing we can do about that now. And nothing we can do before . . ." Quinn stopped himself mid-sentence. "Except maybe Cameron, sort of," Quinn added.

Sentry appeared in front of them. "You called?"

"You read my mind."

"I know what you're thinking. And, yes. We can bring Cameron into the simulation loop, but it will only be for a short time, a millisecond before you leave for the surface. My calculations reveal a 94 percent probability the energy field won't be triggered if she enters just before you leave. That should be enough for a few dozen cycles in the simulator to bring her up to speed on the most important details from your most recent loops."

Quinn smiled, and then Axel screamed. Quinn turned just as the tail of a modified alligator sliced both Axel and Jeremy into two. "Fine. Reset."

The simulation restarted. This time, the simulation dropped them in an underground arena resembling something from *Gladiator*. Quinn and his team bore leather contraptions over their outfits with various sharp weapons but no laser pistols.

At least a dozen beasts filled the stadium. Sentry sat at the top like Caesar, eating grapes with a big smile on his face. He yelled at Quinn through a full fake crowd. "Go on then."

"Assume the stance," Quinn said.

They formed a tight circle, their spines pressed against one another, eyes fixed on the encircling creatures. The beasts prowled, their growls reverberating through the arena. "We strike together," Quinn commanded. "Coordinate your movements, and watch each other's backs."

Quinn deflected a lunging wolf-creature with a wide blade swing. Dr. Green stabbed another, spilling dark blood. Axel and Jeremy, fighting in tandem, executed fluid, strategic moves.

After a narrow escape, they paused. Spotting a slight opening, Quinn whispered, "Wait for it," eyes locked on the creatures.

As the next assault came, Quinn and his team dodged, parried, and returned blows. One creature stumbled, momentarily off balance, and Quinn seized the opportunity, driving his weapon deep into its side. The beast howled and collapsed to the ground.

They continued their dance of blades, each team member finding their rhythm amidst the chaos. With every successful strike, the crowd above roared. Quinn's attention shifted to Sentry, whose eyes never wavered from the fighting.

Just when Quinn thought they were gaining the upper hand, the environment shifted. The ground beneath them trembled, and the walls of the arena shook violently. The once stationary crowd now gasped and screamed as the surroundings morphed into a chaotic spectacle. The entire colosseum split open, revealing a gaping chasm that stretched deep into the abyss.

"What the hell is happening now?" Axel shouted over the deafening noise.

Sentry's voice boomed from above, "I have introduced a twist. Welcome to the second phase of your training."

Quinn and his team leaped away and narrowly avoided

the opening chasm. As the ground stabilized, they found themselves on separate platforms. A batch of more ferocious adversaries joined the creatures and moved toward each team member, surrounding them on all sides.

"We need to regroup," Quinn yelled and scanned the area for any sign of his teammates.

"On it, Boss!" Axel said as he fended off a pair of snarling beasts with his weapon.

Quinn formed a plan in his mind. Each team member had to reach a central platform in the arena, where they could reunite and fight together again. After a few seconds of explanation, they took off to their respective areas.

Quinn jostled between the legs of one of the beasts, avoiding its massive claws. He leaped from platform to platform, each one shaking under his feet. Dr. Green sliced into the heel of the closest creature with a short blade, allowing him to sidestep toward Quinn.

Quinn explained earlier that they had a big advantage over larger creatures. Sure, the beasts could squash them like gnats if they happened to be exposed out in the open, so he told them how to keep out of view. Run in circles, find the corners, and lead the animals into collisions. Axel and Dr. Green got the hang of it, and the team coalesced into a fighting machine.

Once they found their rhythm and the animals were on their posteriors, the stadium vanished, and the group found themselves in a barren desert with the pyramids barely in view.

"Come on, Boss. Now he's just toying with us," Axel said.

Quinn opened his mouth. A flash of light and an awful

wail from somewhere in the distance interrupted him. A dark spot in the sky muted the blinding sun and split the sky into two.

"Drink what you can, and then let's run like hell to the pyramids," Quinn said.

"We'll never make it," Dr. Green replied.

"Maybe not, but this is just a simulation, and Sentry has made it worse. But better to die here than out there," Quinn said.

Axel and Jeremy took out their water pouch and gulped down what they could. Dr. Green followed suit. Once they finished, Axel sprinted forward, and Quinn, Jeremy, and Dr. Green lagged behind in that order.

A short while later, they arrived at the Great Pyramid, panting and drenched in sweat. Quinn drained the last drop of water and tossed it aside, collapsing onto the ground. A momentary spout of dizziness overcame him, but he shook it off and felt for an entrance.

Over the next hour, Quinn and team navigated the traps embedded in the simulation while trying to accomplish their main objective, but Quinn knew even with reverse time dilation, they didn't have forever, and when they landed on the planet for real, the convergence was the wild card that even Sentry couldn't plan for.

Sentry let them earn a few hard-fought wins but gave them enough impossible losses to keep them humble and tired. Eventually, he let them finish on a win and gave them a solid nine hours of compressed time to sleep and regain their mental strength before they left the simulation and attempted their goals in the current loop.

CHAPTER 26

EARTH 2/MULTIVERSE 732, PLANET SURFACE, LOOP 20

THE MOMENT THE team landed on the surface, their expressions shifted. Darkness took up more of the sky than the last time.

"How long do you think we have?" Jeremy asked Quinn.

Dr. Green mumbled something, doing some back-of-the-envelope calculations. "Ten, maybe twelve loops if we're lucky," he said.

Quinn exhaled. "You know what we need to do. Let's make the most of it."

"Ooh. I just got a tingle up my leg. Reminds me of the jungle. Let's do this," Axel replied.

Immediately, the team split in two and headed toward adjacent corners of the Great Pyramid. Quinn and Dr. Green ran left, while Axel and Jeremy sprinted right.

The sandy ground crunched as they marched. "Remember the sequence," Quinn reminded Dr. Green as they approached the pyramid's entrance.

"Move quickly," Quinn said, leading the way.

The dimly lit passageway flickered. Quinn's team retraced their steps until a large chamber containing the beacon appeared, and they stopped.

"I'm not picking up any unusual readings, so you should be good to go," Sentry said in Quinn's ear.

Quinn signaled Dr. Green to enter the chamber. "This better work," Dr. Green said.

Quinn placed the bag containing the spheres on the top of the platform and then removed them from their covering.

On the other corner of the Great Pyramid, Jeremy slid into the chamber following Axel. Both had their hands near their pistols. Over time, they developed a signal before they entered each passageway and into the next chamber. They cleared one corridor after another until they reached the final set they'd been searching for.

"Think they'll be here?" Jeremy asked.

A nearby sound interrupted them. "Who's they?" a voice said from behind.

Jeremy's chest tightened. Axel turned, pistol in hand.

"Easy there. We called you. Remember?"

It took a few seconds for Jeremy's eyes to register. Alternate Quinn and crew stood in front of them.

"And why did you call us?"

Alternate Quinn smiled. "We already met before. A few times. And to answer your question . . ."

Gary interrupted him, "He means the question you're thinking, not the question you just asked."

"Yes, we're in this loop too. We found the same chamber and figured that part out."

Jeremy wondered if Quinn had made it to the other room with Dr. Green yet.

"How much time before they find us?" Jeremy asked.

"Not long," alternate Dr. Green replied.

"Quinn and Dr. Green should be at the beacon. The first time we tried to use it, The Way discovered us. We still need to deactivate it to get off the planet's surface. But before that, I'm assuming you know what we have to do," Jeremy replied.

"The convergence. When I first got here, we discovered they were using the planet to recruit different versions of us for their plan. Once they get a new recruit, they send 'em out to do their bidding. It won't work, but that doesn't mean they won't keep trying," alternate Quinn said.

"If we destroy the beacon, will it stop whatever's happening in the sky?" Jeremy asked.

"What *is* happening?" Axel asked.

"They're accelerating the universal constant for this universe. What we see is just a small expansion of a tiny area nearby in space after their experiments funneling exotic matter into a confined area. We learned the universal constant itself can be modified based on the motion and density of exotic particles."

"Idiots," alternate Dr. Green said.

"How did they manage to recruit anyone to their scheme?" Axel asked.

"With an infinite number of universes, you find an infinite number of idiots," Alternate Quinn said.

"So what's next?" Axel asked.

"There are very large chambers hidden underground. When I arrived at my old timeline, after living it over once I returned, we uncovered more of the truth. That led us to this Earth. We found part of the information in the video archives, other bits we found in research, and the rest we found here," alternate Quinn said.

"What happened to your Tier 1?" Jeremy asked.

"A long story, but the short of it is those people here running around in robes destroyed it. We learned how The Way was trying to extract energy from nearby universe clusters. This is their base," alternate Quinn said.

Axel squinted. "It doesn't seem very well guarded."

"It's well below ground. The surface and just beneath it are a smoke screen. Their strategy involves trapping and enlisting recruits. They run experiments in the underground mid-levels, intending to replicate them across different universes to wreak havoc. They siphon energy here using the spheres," alternate Quinn said.

"Why don't they just hop into a different universe or multiverse?" Jeremy asked.

"They don't like to share, and they don't think others will like it either. They've developed an elaborate way of meddling with society in the hopes of transforming people into pliable dupes who they can control, living in anger and fear," alternate Quinn said.

"Will it work?" Axel asked.

Alternate Quinn exchanged glances with alternate Dr. Green, who then retrieved a small holo-emitter from his pocket and activated it. A three-dimensional diagram appeared between them.

"See this here? They have found a way to draw in energy using the spheres, but it's localized. It can still kill billions and destroy planets in the blink of an eye, but a single multiverse is too much for them to destroy. And as you've already learned, there are an infinite number of multiverses, not just an infinite number of universes in each multiverse," alternate Dr. Green said.

Jeremy remained silent for a moment and then responded. "Is this related to the energy field that activates when we use the spheres?"

"That's it exactly. They designed them to transfer it to wherever they think they need it."

Axel frowned. "Are you saying we shouldn't use them?"

"A discussion for another day, but at a minimum we need to study the spheres' true purpose, which will help us master how they function," Quinn replied.

"I hope this doesn't mean we can't go past warp five," Jeremy said. A small electronic device beeped from Jeremy's satchel. "They've turned off the beacon. We need to go," Jeremy added.

After navigating several corridors, Jeremy and Axel arrived with the alternate team in a large chamber, one Jeremy had seen in an earlier loop. They waited a little over a minute.

Quinn and Dr. Green hurried through the entrance.

"We don't have much time," Quinn said.

Quinn scanned the room. "Good to see you all made it. We've deactivated the beacon, so it won't be long before they find us."

Quinn pulled one of the larger orbs from his satchel. "We can't do what we need to do from here. We'll need to get into orbit above the planet, and this will buy us some time."

Quinn considered his words and what wasn't said. He knew others were on and below the planet. For the plan to work, he'd need to leave them, unsure if saving them was even a possibility.

CHAPTER 27

Earth 2/Multiverse 732, planet surface, loop 20

DOZENS OF ROBED men raced toward Quinn.

Quinn gripped the silver handle, which rested in the up position. "Let's try this again. Here goes nothing," he said and shifted the handle down.

Once the handle met the bottom, it whirred as if something were about to explode. A shock wave flew out from their location and knocked down everything racing toward them.

Quinn gripped the second handle and shifted down. A second wave, this one silent, sent a shimmering light expanding outward that dissipated as it expanded and froze everything except for Quinn's team and their alternates.

Quinn hesitated for a moment and then shifted down on the third handle. Sparks flew from the central panel outward and intersected with the air at a great distance, dancing unevenly and growing in thickness until the sparks resembled thick bolts of lightning.

"Let go of the handle," Dr. Green shouted.

Quinn released his grip. Once free, the electrical bolts reversed direction and shot toward Quinn. He collapsed onto the floor.

The rest of those still unfrozen by time rushed to where Quinn lay on the ground.

"We should loop," Jeremy said.

Dr. Green and his alternate self stared at each other as if processing what had just happened.

"What went wrong?" Axel asked.

"That's what we need to learn before we do anything else. Otherwise, this will just happen again," Dr. Green said.

Another discharge shot toward Quinn's body, and then he vanished.

"Woah! What just happened?" Axel asked.

"Sorry. That was me. There's no time to explain," Sentry said from an indistinct location.

The rest of the group turned in both directions, looking for the point of origin.

"Sentry?" Jeremy said.

"That's right. I'm all around you, using the minerals in the rocks to relay my voice."

"That shouldn't be possible," alternate Quinn said.

"You should know there's almost always a workaround, especially when you have lifetimes to find one."

Alternate Quinn faced the wall. "We need to get off this planet."

The robed men drew closer.

"Not until you tell us where you sent Quinn," Jeremy replied.

"Guys," Gary said as he stared down the men closing on their position.

"What makes you think I sent him anywhere?"

"Answer the question," Axel added.

"I only know why he left and what he went to do, but I can't reveal that now. We need to get off this planet first, so put aside your anger and your ego, and let's leave before I'm the only one of you left."

"We can loop," Jeremy said.

"Not anymore. I saw to that myself. It was the only way. You're going to have to trust me. In less than a minute in real-time, this planet will be completely destroyed, and getting off is just the first thing we have to do. We still need to get to the source and stop The Way from unraveling the fabric of the multiverse," Sentry continued. "And if Quinn doesn't return soon, we might have to face the consequences without him."

Jeremy, Axel, and the alternates exchanged worried glances.

"Okay, let's get off this planet. Lead the way," Jeremy said.

Sentry guided them through a hidden passage as they sprinted through the ancient structures, avoiding the frozen figures along the way.

Amid the chaos, the once serene landscape trembled, sending ripples through every grain of sand and ancient stone. In the distance, stars flickered in random waves against the crimson and violet horizon.

As the seconds ticked by, thunderous booms echoed through the barren landscape. The vibrations intensified. Cracks spiderwebbed across the once pristine ground, fracturing the ancient ruins. Dust and debris spun in the swirling eddies of particles in the howling winds.

In the distant sky, a blue spherical structure blinked into view.

"What is that?" Axel asked.

"We might be too late," Sentry said.

The hidden door in the sand opened, and Kira emerged from underneath wearing traditional ancient Egyptian garb.

Dr. Green squinted. "Have we met before?"

"Get in," she said and disappeared underneath the hatch.

The team followed her instructions and entered the hidden chamber. Inside, an intricate blue spherical device rested on a pedestal.

Jeremy eyed the artifact. "What is that thing?"

"Just something I rigged up," Sentry replied.

A few bright flashes shot out of the sphere and lit up the underground chamber.

"This thing destroyed our home, and it's destroyed others like it," Kira added.

CHAPTER 28

TIER 1, EARTH 2/MULTIVERSE 732, LOOP UNKNOWN, TIME AND DATE UNKNOWN

QUINN OPENED HIS eyes. Cameron stood over him, smiling. "It worked!"

Quinn's head throbbed. His body ached more than he thought possible. He attempted to speak, but his voice failed him. Unconsciousness tugged at him. His head spun. He jostled to the side.

"Try not to move too much," she said.

"What happened?"

The images from the surface flashed into his mind, and for a moment, he couldn't tell what was a memory and what was real.

"Just take it easy for now. I'll brief you once we get you fixed up."

Quinn rested and closed his eyes. When he opened them, more appeared in the room, and he was unsure if he'd fallen asleep. His vision cleared somewhat, but most of the people and objects were still too hazy to identify. Cameron stood in the corner, now in a different outfit than just moments before.

A voice close to him spoke. "He's awake," it said.

Quinn blinked, and his vision cleared. His eyes darted to both sides. Several familiar people he couldn't identify approached. He coughed and then spoke up.

"Cameron. Is that you?"

She stepped forward. Her baby bump was gone. Quinn's chest tightened.

"Something's wrong. Where am I? Or . . ." He paused. "When am I?"

Cameron smiled wider. "Nothing gets past you, does it?"

A fuzzy image moved toward him in the room just low enough for him not to picture it clearly, and he noticed a few new lines near Cameron's eyes.

"We brought you here. We just couldn't do it immediately."

A large attractive man who appeared in his early forties approached. "Good to finally see you in the flesh," the man said.

"And who are you?"

"I think you know who I am."

The voice, Quinn recognized. "No way."

"Way, my friend. Way. Not The Way, of course, but *way* as in the sense of yes in the affirmative."

"Sentry?"

The man smiled. "Way. And since you've been gone, I fabricated this body. And it's not just me."

"What happened to the rest of the team? And what about our alternates?"

Cameron's face dropped. She opened her mouth to say

something, but a small child crawled up onto the bed where Quinn was lying. "Are you my daddy?" the young boy asked.

Cameron smiled, caressed the boy's head, and stared at Quinn. "We need to go somewhere and speak in private."

"It's going to be alright," Sentry added.

Cameron gave her arm to Quinn, who grasped it gently and leveraged himself into an upright position. As the room settled, he paused until the spinning stopped and the surrounding figures focused.

Quinn adjusted his position until he was satisfied he wouldn't collapse onto the table. He then pressed his feet firmly on the ground and pushed himself up slowly until he was in a standing position. His heart still raced, but he inhaled deeply and focused on his breath, pushing aside the thought of passing out.

"That feeling you have will go away soon. We've just injected you with the latest version of the nanites we've been working on," a woman in a white lab coat said.

Quinn's muscles tensed and then relaxed. His breathing slowed to its typical pace along with his heartbeat.

"Follow me," Cameron said.

All at once, Quinn's vision focused. The room was clearer than before. What troubled him more was that he didn't recognize anyone except for Cameron.

"This way," she motioned.

Quinn followed. Sentry strolled alongside him. Once outside the room, the familiar hallways of Tier 1 appeared. His eyes focused more as he used them, almost as if he had enhanced vision. A few subtle changes in the walls and doors stood out. With little effort, his eyes zoomed in on newly uncovered features.

"How long have I been unconscious?" Quinn asked.

Cameron approached their quarters, and Quinn stepped in. Sentry followed. She closed the door behind them, her eyes meeting Quinn's. "A little over five years," she finally replied.

Quinn's knees wobbled. The room spun again. Sentry reached out, steadying him.

"Five years?" Quinn said, pausing. "What happened? How?"

"There was a lot we didn't understand about the technology we were using. Bringing you back wasn't simple, and the time distortions only made it more complicated. We had to be careful or we could have lost you forever."

"Bringing me back? From what? From where?"

Sentry's almost human eyes met Quinn's. "The universe you left is not the one you find now. Changes have taken place, things have shifted, but the danger, the core problem that sent you into the multiverse, still looms."

"You didn't answer my question. We had a plan. What happened?"

The entrance door rattled, stealing their attention. The young boy bolted toward Quinn and then wrapped his arms around Quinn's waist. He inspected the boy, saying nothing.

He viewed the boy's eyes and head, down to his gangly limbs. Tranquility replaced Quinn's brief disorientation. "I think those nanites are kicking in," he said, smiling.

Quinn picked up the boy into his arms. "You do look like me. I'm sure whatever happens, we'll have a lot to talk about. But we've got some grownup things to discuss first. Do you have a place where you can go and play? It won't be long. I promise."

CHAPTER 29

Earth 2/Multiverse 1, Central Park, NYC, 2063

ALTERNATE QUINN SCANNED the Central Park landscape below with his eyes, his face the same age as when he arrived from over forty years in the past. The park had expanded, its boundaries reaching out to embrace the city.

Towering trees rose to meet the sky, their thick canopies sheltering a myriad of life forms. Among them were both biological birds and their mechanical counterparts, their chirps and electronic trills blending into the urban biodiversity.

Above the ground, floating botanical gardens hovered over the shimmering lakes. Their roots dipped into the crystal-clear water. Families congregated on the plush, emerald carpet of grass under the gentle shade of the trees. Laughter echoed as children frolicked and chased lifelike robotic butterflies.

A figure emerged from one of the sidewalks leading to alternate Quinn's position. A few more steps revealed a woman he recognized immediately, around forty, he knew, but the color in her cheeks and lack of lines made her appear in her twenties.

She wore a sleek, form-fitting jumpsuit that changed hues with the angle of the sun. A delicate collar extended upward from the neckline, wrapping gracefully around her neck. An intricate pattern of conductive silver embroidery ran down her arms and contrasted with the main color of the jumpsuit, adding a touch of complexity to an otherwise minimalist design.

"You made it," the woman smiled.

"Tell me it worked," alternate Quinn said.

Her smile grew. "In this timeline it did. This means when I return you, the issue will be resolved in your cluster of universes. The threat will always remain for other timelines and perhaps in my future."

He considered her words. "And what about the other Quinn?"

"I can track his return home, but beyond that, it's unclear. You selected his timeline because it closely resembles yours before the paths diverged. The chances of success in his future closely match yours upon your return."

Quinn relaxed for the first time since he arrived. "How long do I have?"

"Since we modified the spheres, we've been able to buy you about five minutes, and then you'll need to return."

"Is Cameron here?" alternate Quinn asked.

Several people stepped forward from behind the nearby shrubs. "We're all here," a woman with fine lines and silver hair said.

Alternate Quinn squinted, inspecting the dozen or so people that had just come into view. "You can't be?"

"That's right. I'm Cameron, and still your wife."

Aside from the silver hair, she appeared roughly the same age as the woman he knew to be his daughter.

"Nanites work wonders on the skin," she said.

"So we found a way to cheat death," alternate Quinn stated.

"Since the first days of modern medicine. And I hope it continues. There's nothing more powerful than the human mind and spirit," she replied.

"And what about the defensive mechanisms we put in place to prevent The Way from converging multiverses? I'm assuming it's held all this time."

Quinn's daughter paused for a moment and then finally answered, "It's held, for now. There were potential problems that came up, and I'll give you some of the potential solutions to them now. But there are always more minefields that need to be overcome. Before I explain more about those, I want to show you what you and your team managed to accomplish. Take my hand."

Quinn grabbed her hand, and instantly their surroundings changed. "One of the technological advances we've made is the ability to share selected memories with whoever wants to experience them. The device you're touching uses the neural pathways to directly communicate them to you."

The setting of the park transformed into what Quinn assumed was a point in the past, and his perspective shifted as if he were seeing through her eyes. A few images of memories flashed around him of thirty-year-old news broadcasts, her past but Quinn's future.

In one clip, a commentator discussed an astronomical event that threatened to impact Earth. The memory forwarded several weeks. The same anchorman discussed how the Array company had once again rescued mankind and prevented the apocalypse.

The memory paused with the news commentator mid-sentence, as her son materialized within it. "You did that," she cut in before letting the next scene play out.

Several more sequences flashed of areas around the globe still suffering from corruption and poverty, though not as severe as alternate Quinn remembered before the supernova. The images jumped to a year later. A round table appeared in a large conference hall. A sign hung on the wall of Palais des Nations, which Quinn knew was a UN meeting room in Geneva, Switzerland. Her memory continued as thinkers around the world discussed their solutions and the shifting political and global landscape in response to Quinn's action.

A few more sequences played out and accelerated until they brought Quinn to her present time, Quinn's future. The memories vanished, and he found himself staring at her. "As you can see, you've made a big difference." She paused and turned, lowering her head slightly. "The biggest threat is in our future. And it's not what you think."

"What do you mean?"

"What we've learned since Sentry catapulted you into your future is the reason The Way targeted your multiverse, your universe."

"Isn't the strategy to create chaos and manipulate events to gain control?"

"Something like that, yes. But they don't target every timeline or every multiverse."

She motioned at a futuristic holo, and lines formed in the air, what Quinn took to be countless timeliness and possibilities. She tossed them aside with her fingers.

"They've used advanced algorithms to locate great chasms, divergences within the timelines and multiverse. If a chasm is great enough, it represents a location ripe for their intervention."

"And let me guess, my timeline is one of them."

"You are the divergence. When your mind shot into your father's body, the other Quinn's didn't, the one you called across the multiverse for help. His future is much less certain. There are forces in his world that could influence him to take a dark turn, and that's what The Way is hoping for."

Quinn reflected on his daughter's words, and then his eyes widened. It made sense that the other Quinn would be influenced by The Way. From what he knew, the original Quinn didn't return to see his family. Instead, Tier 1 flung him into another world where an evil version of himself had built a different array for reasons he still didn't fully comprehend. Nonetheless, the construct from that vessel remained active.

Quinn wondered if Sentry was manipulating things behind the scenes for some unknown purpose and if he'd been responsible for the original sabotage on the array.

"Is Sentry on our side, or is he responsible for the original sabotage? I know The Way was involved, but is he working for them?"

She put her hand on Quinn's shoulder and smiled. "He's been honest with you, and from what I know about your possible futures, he's never led the other Quinn astray."

Quinn's view of Central Park returned with its harmonious integration with nature. The five minutes he was there were timeless.

Quinn's eyes took in the rich shades of green and the

bubbling of the crystal-clear lakes, mingling with children's laughter and the faint rustling of the towering trees. He inhaled the sweet scent of blooming flowers and the fresh aroma of damp earth, and then he refocused on why and how he'd arrived in the first place.

"He sent me here for a reason. That was part of the plan, wasn't it? To get some piece of knowledge from the future so we could stop The Way's futile attempt to rebirth their dying world."

After he spoke those words, one thing occurred to him that he hadn't considered before. "We estimated how far I could travel in the future, and using an algorithm, Sentry sent me to the closest line of my current predicted future to save on exotic matter. But how far exactly can I go?" Quinn asked.

"Ah. You've hit upon the real question, the one that is the true reason behind The Way's lust for more energy."

"What do you mean?"

"Their universe was dying due to the use and creation of exotic matter. I could provide the formula, but self-discovery will keep you honest. Essentially, you can create exotic matter in the same way as matter and antimatter. However, this process accelerates the universe's expansion rate, a phenomenon your scientists have already observed with galaxies expanding faster than expected."

Quinn's eyes widened. Images of what The Way must have done fluttered around in his mind. "They're speeding up entropy because of time travel to the future!"

"That's exactly right. It consumes much more energy to travel forward because the past already exists. The future has infinite possibilities. The past is limited, especially in the sense of the conglomeration of universes and multiverses, which is a discussion for another day. The main thing is that you came here for something. I need to give that to you, and then I'm sending you back."

She tapped his shoulder, and a glass-like bubble enveloped them. Before he understood what was happening, a hypertube swirled to their location and enveloped the bubble.

They shot off at incredible speeds. The landscape of Central Park blurred into streaks of green and blue, mingling with the rich gold of the late afternoon sun. The scenery around them changed rapidly. Before he could adjust, they emerged on the edge of the city skyline, staring at a massive edifice that towered above the tallest skyscrapers.

They came to a stop. Alternate Quinn gazed around himself. The location was somewhere in a shimmering pillar of cascading lights and dynamic designs. Walkways floated between sections, and transparent elevators shot up and down the vast height. People crawled like ants, and their tasks harmonized with the structure's rhythm.

"This is where you'll get the answers you need."

Inside, vines and cables ran alongside one another in a blend of organic and modern designs. Screens bloomed like flowers from walls and floors. An intricate central dais with a lustrous surface awaited them.

As they approached, a crystalline entity rose from the platform. "This contains the accumulated knowledge and experiences of countless timelines across the multiverse cluster."

Quinn's fingers touched the crystal. Upon impact, memories, images, and sensations took hold. Understandings of

The Way, of their strategies and flaws, of the intrinsic links between multiverses and their shared fate flooded into him.

"You now carry with you the essence of what makes this timeline stand against The Way," she said. "Use it wisely."

Before he could reply, a sudden pull yanked on him, and the environment faded into darkness.

CHAPTER 30

Earth 2/Multiverse 732, planet surface, loop unknown

ALTERNATE QUINN MATERIALIZED in the cavern he assumed was the present time. A tingling overtook his body. His surroundings shifted, and he found himself inhaling dry, dusty air. The faint scent of aged parchment and torch oils hung in the still atmosphere. Several figures surrounded him, though they were still fuzzy.

The sand-covered floor crunched beneath his feet. A subtle echo resounded from another chamber. His eyes adjusted to the soft, golden light within the catacomb.

Finally, the transport bubble dissolved completely, sloughing off around him like a translucent shell. Meticulous hieroglyphs lining the walls popped into clear view. The rest of his team surrounded him, as did the members of his alternate self's team, including Jeremy. But Quinn was gone.

"What just happened? Where'd you go, and where's *our* Quinn?" Jeremy asked.

Axel's face dropped. "What the hell, man? Are you on

our side or what? If I find out you've done something to our Quinn . . ."

A crackle cut Axel off. Alternate Quinn opened his hand. "This is part of the reason why I called you. I have what we need now to create the barrier to shut down The Way's convergence funnel. I had to travel into the future to get it."

Dr. Green's face tightened, and he stepped forward. "Where's our Quinn?"

The expressions of the rest of the team hinted at similar questions. Alternate Quinn opened his mouth to answer. Footsteps interrupted them.

Kira blazed through the entrance, holding a torch. Several people followed close behind, including her father, Ubuntu.

Jeremy gazed at Kira, certain he'd seen her before. The expression on her face made him think she'd definitely seen him, and then she gave what he swore was a brief smile.

"I've been in constant communication with your AI, Sentry. We couldn't risk the others learning of the full plan, so Sentry only gave enough details to point you in the right direction and keep The Way looking elsewhere."

Kira turned toward alternate Quinn. He unveiled a futuristic contraption and planted it on the floor, twisting the top portion of the rod until it clicked into place.

Axel leaned over and whispered in Jeremy's ear, "I think she likes you, bro."

Jeremy turned and squinted, giving Axel a look that made Axel smile. Jeremy turned his attention to alternate Quinn. Numerous light filaments burst from the device anchored in the Earth. They formed a loop from the ground and expanded outward.

"All we have to do now is wait," alternate Quinn said.

"Do you know anything about this?" Jeremy asked Dr. Green.

Dr. Green shook his head. Jeremy turned to alternate Dr. Green. "What about you?" Jeremy asked.

Alternate Dr. Green glanced at alternate Quinn. Jeremy assumed they wanted to communicate how much they wished to reveal.

The long rod, which Jeremy assumed was a sensor mast, snapped to life.

"Give it a minute. I don't think we're going to have to wait for long," alternate Quinn said.

CHAPTER 31

Earth 2/Multiverse 732, Tier 1, 2030

QUINN WATCHED AS Cameron took their son out of the room. The presence of the nanites in his system made it easier to process information and emotions, but the massive gap of time still clouded his thoughts.

Sentry moved closer. The metallic sheen of his body reflected the dim room lights. "While you were gone, the multiverse continued to destabilize, and the effects rippled across every dimension in the local cluster."

Quinn thought for a moment. "But we knew that would happen. That's why I'm here. That's what you told me. Just send me into the future to get the missing frequency. Did anyone else see the micro-shuttle when it arrived during the explosion?"

Quinn ran his fingers through his hair, and the memory of their original plan flashed in his mind. "We were supposed to stabilize it. There was a device . . ."

"Ah, yes. Well. We knew the planet would be consumed before you could return. The good news is that the patchwork fix we implemented stopped the convergence, at least up until now. That allowed us to use the spheres to navigate away from the planet in Tier 1. Just not all of us. With the beacon partially deactivated, we were able to travel into the future using the spheres. I discovered the intel you provided in the last loop from the construct," Sentry said.

Cameron returned and approached Quinn, shoving something onto his arm. "This contraption will sync up with the energy field of any spheres in the area. It will do the same thing to the beacon and deactivate the frequency causing the convergence."

"And you're sure you have the right frequency?" Quinn asked.

There was a moment of silence. "You don't know. Do you?"

"It's the best we could do given the amount of time we had. It should work."

"Should?"

"There's a 72 percent probability," Sentry said.

Quinn raised his eyebrows. "I guess it could be worse."

"It all comes down to this, at least in this universe," Cameron said.

"There *is* another option," Sentry added.

Cameron leered at Sentry as if he had exposed a secret. He didn't elaborate on it.

"I can't stay here," Quinn replied. As soon as the words came out of his mouth, he rethought what he had just said. "Or *can* I? Maybe I can loop time until we get the percentages up."

Cameron shook her head. "We've learned a lot more about time travel and the spheres during your absence. You don't have enough juice. You used up most of it on your trip here. The inverse square law, remember? The level of energy needed to create more is too much for us."

"We're still holding back The Way in this timeline. You have enough residual energy to return and do some short loops, but after that, you'll need a recharge. You can do that once you successfully stop the convergence and return to Earth. Unfortunately for us here, we're cut off from the rest of the node network, so our supply is limited."

"Can you measure exactly how much exotic matter I have?" Quinn asked.

Sentry ran a scanner down Quinn's body. "You've got enough for a few dozen short-term loops after you return, but that's it. You depleted most of the residual energy with that maneuver we pulled in the pyramid. Normally the spheres would do the job of transporting you with no impact on your body's reserves. Unfortunately, I had to use some of your residual dark matter to transport the microshuttle to you. It might have looked like you vanished in a small explosion to everyone else who was in your position," Sentry said.

"What about my alternate self? Did he make it back?" the moment Quinn asked, he realized it was a silly question.

"You're still probably not up to your full self just yet, but he's in another timeline. He's dead, along with everyone else on the planet's surface in this timeline. Fortunately, Tier 1 is tethered to you with the use of the spheres."

"Maybe he passed through the loop portal. He could be alive if he loops to my location again. Once I return, it should change this loop."

Quinn's brain hurt more than usual as he thought about it.

"The alternate you may have technology we don't know about. He went to the future. You can ask him when you return. In either case, we don't have much time. You'll need to run the simulation to learn how to implant and activate the frequency, and then we'll need to send you back. That residual dark matter will come in handy when we pull all of you out of there. It will increase the probability of success. That's another reason why it's better not to risk any loops in the current timeline. The best we can do is the simulator," Cameron said.

The young boy shuffled in and ran to grab Quinn with his small hand. Quinn wanted to get to know him better, but he also felt guilty, like he'd been an absent father without any intention of doing so.

Quinn then shook the feeling, considering how the timeline would change as part of the connected loop. "Wait a second. You're not in the loop. This means . . ."

"Not what you think," Cameron finished.

Quinn was about to ask how, but Sentry beat him to it with an image of the convergence across nearby timeline clusters.

"I see what you mean. If I stop the convergence, the drain of exotic matter from all the nearby clusters will stop."

"Exactly. The spheres allow transport into nearby timelines through the creation of singularities. It can't go backward in the same multiverse, but as you theorized in your time, there is more than one multiverse."

Quinn analyzed his options and the implications once again. "But you'll be safe."

Cameron smiled. "We'll be safe. As will all surrounding

timelines within our multiverse. And when you return, so will we because . . ."

At that moment, it occurred to him. "The explosion expanded the loop! Tier 1 is in the loop!"

Cameron smiled again. "That's exactly right. We still had to wait for you to get here. Since your alternate also needed to return, we couldn't loop from the start. You both need to be in the same timeline so both of you can simultaneously use knowledge from the future," Cameron said.

A loud, high-low tone echoed in Tier 1, interrupting them. "No time to waste. We've made the simulation interface a bit more user-friendly while you've been gone. Run through it five times, and then we'll yank you out," Sentry said.

Quinn found himself in a digital replica of the pyramid. Kira, Axel, Jeremy, both versions of Dr. Green, and the others stood around him. The thick and damp air clung to his skin. Cold stones lay under his feet, and dust filled his lungs. The spheres thrummed, ushering in the simulation.

CHAPTER 32

EARTH 2/ MULTIVERSE 732, PLANET SURFACE, LOOP 20

PARTICLES OF ANCIENT dust stirred in the air. They reflected faint light as they moved. Deep within the cavern, large stones shifted, emitting low sounds. Axel stopped arguing.

The ground trembled from deep beneath the cavern floor, and an intensely bright energy sphere emerged.

"That must be him," alternate Quinn said.

The orb ascended, illuminating the vast space around it. Within a short radius of the sphere, the sleek, distinct shape of the micro-shuttle's exterior and polished surfaces appeared.

The rumbling ceased, and the hatch opened. Quinn unfolded himself, standing upright. "We don't have much time. You know where we need to go," Quinn said, looking into Kira's eyes.

Jeremy stared blankly.

"We're only going to get one shot at this. Hurry," Quinn said.

"You mean we're not going to get another twenty tries?" Jeremy asked.

"The both of us spent most of our residual exotic matter traveling to and from the future. It's too dangerous to risk another loop. We have to assume this is the last one."

Axel's suspicious glare at alternate Quinn finally softened. "Told ya," alternate Quinn said.

A few feet away, Quinn retrieved a device from his pocket and handed it to Kira. "It's modified from your designs, and it has an added filter from the data we've collected over the loops."

Kira's eyes widened. "You brought this from the future."

"In a nutshell."

Quinn paused before explaining, "We need to insert it at the exact point of the convergence." He glanced at alternate Quinn. "We're synchronizing our actions."

Alternate Quinn forced a smile. "No mistakes."

Both Quinns slowed down and examined the interface more closely. Alternate Quinn tapped a timer on his wrist that Quinn's vision relayed in front of him thanks to the nanites now coursing through his veins.

As the group moved, the cavern's acoustic tricks intensified. For a moment, Quinn thought beasts were running into the entrance.

Axel, still hesitant, led the way. Jeremy glanced at the device in Kira's hand. "So you insert this and it stops the whole thing? Just like that?" Jeremy asked.

Quinn shot him a glance. "In theory. If we're lucky, it'll reverse some of the damage as well."

"I think there's going to be an awful lot of angry robed men after us," Jeremy said.

"We can take 'em. But what's up with those robes anyways? You'd think they would've found some better outfits by now with all those time loops," Axel replied.

Alternate Quinn led the way, with Quinn and Kira close behind, moving in unison as they approached the nexus. Suddenly, a blast echoed through the cavern. Dust and debris fell from the ceiling.

Alternate Quinn shouted over the noise, "They definitely know we're here now."

Kira clutched the device close to her chest and quickened her pace. "Almost there! Do whatever you can to stop them," she shouted out to her father.

Ubuntu stepped forward, his followers increasing in numbers, serving as a protective shield around the group. Jeremy and Axel took up defensive positions. Echoing footsteps grew louder. Soon, dark silhouettes emerged from the shadows until they were right up against Ubuntu's men.

"More of those badly dressed robed dudes. Time to break out a can of whoop-ass," Axel said.

Both Dr. Greens and Jeremy fell behind Axel and brandished their guns, aiming at those running toward them.

Quinn glanced at alternate Quinn. "Same time, remember?"

The two Quinns aligned their steps toward the vortex, a chaotic blend of colors.

"Quinn, can you hear me?" Sentry said in Quinn's ear.

"Loud and clear. Glad I don't have to pretend like I'm talking to someone in the room for a change. What's up?"

"You need to delay the maneuver for another ninety seconds. We're monitoring the exotic particle energy fluctuations from up here, and based on the new information you provided, it's going to take that long to reach the required frequency for the engines to sync up with new energy emitters."

A firefight unfolded near the entrance. A dozen of

Ubuntu's men joined in the fight, but several large creatures trailed the accompanying guards.

"I'm not sure if we have that long," Quinn said.

"I'll see if we can buy you some time," Kira said.

"We'll try to divert some of their energy readings from here," Sentry told Quinn in his ear.

The vortex grew louder, pulling Quinn closer as he struggled against it. The countdown on the device ticked down. "Almost there," he said.

Jeremy unleashed a series of shots toward the oncoming robed figures. The sharp pop of each one echoed through the cavern. As the countdown neared its end, more of Ubuntu's men joined in battle. Half of them carried menacing pistols and targeted the creatures.

"Man, those are ugly beasts," Dr. Green said.

Once Ubuntu's barrier backed him, Axel unleashed a barrage of attacks. The cavern's corridors amplified each shot, and the explosions obscured much of the room in a cloud of smoke and dust.

"Now!" Quinn shouted.

Both Quinns approached the spinning mass. Suddenly, a massive jolt rocked the cavern and threw them off their coordinated efforts. Quinn's knees buckled, and he dropped the device. Kira came up from behind him and caught it before it could hit the floor.

Quinn steadied himself, clutched the device from Kira's hands, and stood up. Once he found his footing, both Quinn's plunged the object into the heart of the vortex. A blinding explosion and deafening silence followed. For a moment, everything stood still.

When his senses returned, a gaping chasm in the cavern

floor stood in the vortex's place, the edges of which still emitted faint wisps of colored smoke. The cavern walls glittered as if they had been polished, and robed figures covered in dust lay scattered around.

Kira approached Quinn with a look of relief on her face. "Did we do it?"

Alternate Quinn stepped forward, surveying the scene. "We did something, alright."

Jeremy joined them. "The robed guys aren't moving, and there's a big hole in the ground where the convergence was funneling the exotic matter, so I think we did what we came here to do."

"You getting all this, Sentry?" Quinn asked.

CHAPTER 33

Earth 2/Multiverse 732, planet surface, loop 20

A SHORT WHILE later, Jeremy sat at a table in an underground cavern with Kira. "Is there any chance you'd consider coming with us?" Jeremy asked.

Kira's face softened. "As much as I love my home and my people, I have been thinking about doing some traveling."

Jeremy smiled, but he stopped it before it grew too large. "Your father won't be upset?"

"My father's a strong man, and he wants me to live my life."

"And your people?"

"I'm sure they'll miss me, like my father. But we'll keep in touch."

"The multiverse is a big place," Jeremy replied.

"It's smaller than you think."

Kira placed her hand on Jeremy's. "So how many times did you go through the loop without me?" Jeremy asked.

"Just enough to want to come with you."

Large tremors rumbled through the room and then

quickly subsided. The door burst open, and Jeremy tensed, preparing to face whatever came through the door.

Axel stood tall, casting a shadow behind him. "You two lovebirds about ready to go? I've got orders from Boss to pick you up in the shuttle."

Jeremy relaxed but didn't immediately reply. He toggled his attention between Kira and Axel before finally replying, "We'll meet you at the rendezvous point in a few minutes."

In their remaining time, Kira discussed how her people navigated their survival, including some daily rituals that helped keep them together. It wasn't much, but in the short time they spoke, Jeremy already had a sense of her connection to the community and her intense gratitude for the small things most people overlooked.

Jeremy's contributions didn't stop him from feeling lost recently, but Kira cleared the fog that once weighed heavily on him.

On Tier 1, Quinn briefed Sentry on all the information he learned from 2030. Sentry combined that with the details he collected from Alternate Quinn's journey much farther in the future and the nanites Quinn had received that were still coursing through his body.

With the new intel, Sentry updated the construct's algorithms. But he wasn't the only one working tirelessly on the new data. Dr. Green burst through the door holding a clunky contraption connected to a small digital interface. "You won't believe what I just discovered!"

Quinn smiled. "Let me guess, a way to measure the residual exotic matter I can use to mentally time travel."

Dr. Green frowned. "Well, you're no fun."

A second later, his frown broke, and the exuberance gleamed on his face once again. "Well, yes. Exactly. I used the information I learned from the loop portal to recalibrate some of the equipment Sentry constructed."

He continued on, giving a long-winded explanation that went over even Quinn's head. While he did, Quinn wondered what the future versions of Cameron and Sentry must've missed. Quinn smiled back. "I'm so glad we have you."

Quinn eventually coaxed Dr. Green to his study, where Quinn made him sit down so he could digest the new information. The next hour disappeared as Dr. Green kept Quinn entranced with more ideas until they uncovered something unexpected.

"Is what I'm seeing correct?" Quinn asked.

Dr. Green's face dropped, letting a moment pass before saying, "Afraid so."

Quinn ran his finger down a couple of lines of math and then compared what he was seeing to the screen. "That's roughly five months. There has to be another way."

"Let's bring it to Sentry and let him run the calculations."

Quinn activated Sentry's interface. Quinn explained the current situation and the rough estimate they calculated before they could return home through the singularity.

"Five months, you say? Let me run some simulations and find a workaround."

Quinn glanced at Dr. Green's invention. "If that contraption can truly measure the residual exotic matter, then maybe we can find a way to optimize its usage."

A ding signaled Sentry's completion. "There's no way around it. The shielding recalibration will need to be perfect before we return. Even a tiny variation will put Tier 1 in the wrong multiverse."

Quinn moved to the interface. "Sentry, scan for more anomalies and any options that might help. And get the team ready. We've got a lot of prep work to do."

As they delved into the exotic matter measurement device, Quinn's thoughts drifted to Cameron's due date.

In one of the subcommand rooms, obscure gadgets and devices surrounded Cameron in her makeshift lab. Her fingers danced over the holographic keyboard, sifting through lines of code and schematics.

The news of the delay startled her. It wasn't just her pregnancy timeline at stake, but the entire mission. The team had to recalibrate the exotic matter, or they might not be able to make it home at all.

Cameron thought of numerous scenarios where they ended up staying another five years like Quinn had explained upon his return. It wouldn't be the same outcome. At least they'd nixed their enemy for the foreseeable future.

She dismissed the dire possibilities and realized an opportunity. While they had the spheres, she knew looping time used exotic matter on a much grander scale. Something she'd seen in some of her calculations hinted at a phantom echo of spent exotic matter. The clue might just be enough to repurpose and channel back into the subnodes.

Cameron's eyes widened and realized the misinstalled array panels they discovered during the meteor storm held another solution. If she could harness even a fraction of that spent exotic matter, they might just have enough for short emergency jumps or, at the very least, localized temporal alterations. But the math suggested it might be much more than that.

With the array, they spun up mankind's energy supply by orders of magnitude. But as the understanding of how to travel through time and across the multiverse grew, so did the knowledge of how much power they needed. With what both Quinns discovered from the future, the energy requirements were off the charts and were the real reason The Way sought both the direct consumption of energy from other universes and timelines, but it also hinted at the reason they sought to sow conflict in whatever world they touched.

Cameron opened a link to Quinn's console. "I think I've found something. Can you route some of that residual exotic matter to my lab? Just a small fraction. I want to run some tests."

Quinn hesitated for a moment. "Did you find something?"

Cameron explained the details of her data over the next few minutes. Quinn remained silent until she finished.

"I'll reroute some to one of the subnode valves. I'll also have Sentry update his algorithm to see what he says, but if this does what you think it will, it sounds like a game changer."

Minutes later, she received the notification from Sentry that he'd routed the exotic matter to the sub-node. She immediately switched on her equipment. Her hands trembled as she adjusted the microscopic settings on the quantum manipulator, a cool new tool that Sentry constructed with the details they'd gleaned from Quinn's five-year-jump to the future.

The quantum manipulator purred, and the display flashed. Slowly, she transferred some residual exotic matter.

The readings on the monitor fluctuated wildly for a moment and then stabilized. Cameron clenched her fists and then made a few more mental calculations. What followed was a spike in the algorithm that matched her theoretical models.

Once they'd gotten word, Quinn and Dr. Green rushed in to see the results. They entered just as a filament of exotic matter synced with the quantum manipulator and became visible on the holo-emitter.

Quinn smiled, and he immediately patched a message into Sentry's construct. Sentry materialized into the room, reminding Quinn of the *Star Trek TNG* episode where the holodeck character, Moriarty, took control of the ship.

Sentry stared back at Quinn as if reading his mind. "Based on these findings, this could dramatically accelerate our energy capabilities and open new possibilities for localized temporal interventions," Sentry said.

Over the next several hours, Sentry worked closely with Dr. Green and Cameron. Eventually, Jeremy and Quinn took up logistical tasks and coordinated efforts both on Tier 1 and what remained on the surface.

Hours turned into days, and after a week on the surface, Sentry alerted Quinn to a breakthrough.

"Let Jeremy and the rest of the team know. Set up a briefing in one hour," Quinn said.

A few pyramids down from Quinn's location, Kira and Jeremy stepped out of the underground cavern, pausing to look at the sky.

Kira gazed over at Jeremy. "This place and the people here will always be a part of me, but I think I'm ready for the next chapter."

Jeremy smiled. "And we're ready for you to be a part of it." They held hands and strolled toward the rendezvous point.

An hour later, Quinn and Sentry's avatar gathered at the

head of the large conference table in the subcommand room, flanked by Kira and Jeremy on one side and Dr. Green and Axel on the other.

"Alright. Sentry found something."

Sentry turned on the holo-emitter, showing a complex model of Tier 1 with linked data streams. Before, the computer systems were not connected, but Sentry made a way to link them through a middle path with a buffer to isolate each part if needed. Dr. Green, Cameron, and Quinn developed the strategy after heated discussions and heeded warnings from Quinn's future counterparts.

"Based on the calculations and experiments conducted by Dr. Green and Cameron, I've recalibrated the exotic matter measurement device. It could give us new energy capabilities that far exceed our initial estimates. It's orders of magnitude greater than the antimatter subnodes provide to create our exotic matter," Sentry said.

Dr. Green added, "In simple terms, we could use the exotic matter faster and more efficiently."

"It's a big step, but we still have a lot of work to turn this theoretical advantage into a practical one, and we'll need to do it in secret. Our primary use for this will be to build a reserve and to keep an eye out for incursions by The Way from other multiverses."

"Don't tell me we're going to become the multiverse police," Jeremy said.

"Hell no. I could care less what other people are doing in the multiverse as long as what they do doesn't risk total annihilation. And I don't mind having a bit of fun if we do it right. The sensors won't be sensitive enough anyway to pick up on that. The process uses residual exotic matter from multiverse incursions within certain multiversal coordinates. But those incursions don't have to be planet killers to shave off some of their spent energy," Quinn said.

"So we're using their weapon against them," Axel said.

"More like using the weapon's energy to construct a shield while amassing a separate reserve," Quinn replied.

"Reminds me of what bank scammers used to do in the old days when they shaved off fractions of a cent for each transaction over millions of transactions," Axel added.

Cameron smiled. "That's exactly what we're doing, only we're doing it with exotic matter. The energy requirements for forward time travel are tremendous. But like anything, there's always waste. We found a way to repurpose that into something usable. It's not much, just a fraction of a percent, so they won't notice and won't care."

"At least until they get smacked in the face if they ever try to hit us again."

"You think it will be enough?" Axel asked.

"We found a way to stop them here. I'm sure they'll adapt, and so will we. We'll know if and when they're coming, and we'll have a leg up in our defenses if need be. This offers more than energy and protection. It gives us the ability to probe in return. We just have to make sure we put in safeguards to prevent the strategy from backfiring and creating a culture that does the same thing that they do," Quinn said.

"And that's the real challenge, isn't it? Keeping ourselves from becoming the very thing we're fighting against," Dr. Green added.

Sentry's holographic form flickered. "A delicate balance to maintain. But it's the one we have to pursue—harnessing this power responsibly while pushing against The Way's attempts to dominate the infinite multiverses."

Axel squinted. Quinn sensed his residual suspicion of Sentry, and if he were being honest with himself, he had a few lingering doubts as well, and not just about Sentry. Still, Quinn knew they had won the battle, but was more concerned with the longer-term war.

Quinn continued, "The plans we craft now have to be resilient, able to adapt as situations change. Every one of us plays a critical role. We have to be flexible, innovative, and, above all, united."

Even as he spoke those words, he knew he'd have trouble completely buying into that "united" thing while he had lingering doubts. He suspected Cameron could see the concern on his face. As a leader, he wanted to project confidence despite his misgivings. Adding safeguards would help him with that, which he committed to do with the current plan.

Once they finished the meeting, Sentry coordinated all automated actions while the rest of them set up the remaining hardware updates to Tier 1 and the planet's surface.

Hours turned into days and then weeks. Before long, they'd polished off the last few updates and spent the better part of the next week brushing up on knowledge from their new upgrades.

CHAPTER 34

TIER 1, EARTH 2/MULTIVERSE 732, LOOP 20 A FEW MONTHS LATER

CAMERON BURST INTO the comms room, grimacing and holding her belly. "Something's wrong."

Quinn rushed over. "Dr. Green, get someone in here."

Cameron winced. Sweat beaded on her face and trickled down. Quinn took one of her hands, and she squeezed. "This can't be it. It's too soon."

Dr. Green called two med techs over the comms. A short while later, one of them assisted Cameron on top of a stretcher, and the other scanned her vitals.

"It is a little early, but I'm not seeing any signs of trauma, other than the fact that you are in labor, that is."

"It's only thirty-four weeks," she replied.

Quinn felt momentarily guilty he hadn't tried harder to convince Cameron to stay home. He knew why he hadn't, but found it difficult not to second-guess his choice.

The med tech shifted as she checked some vital signs and

reviewed a few numbers. "Looks like you're going to have a healthy preemie," she said, smiling.

Quinn rushed over once she was settled. Once he did, Cameron gripped his hand harder than she'd done earlier as she screamed. "I'm here," he said. Both med techs continued checking her vitals and ushered everyone else out of the room. Over the next several hours, Quinn stood by Cameron's side as she went through all the stages of childbirth. Once their son was sound asleep and the med techs left, fatigue overcame them, and they passed out from exhaustion.

Sometime later, the baby's faint cry pierced the stillness. Cameron's eyes sprung open, and she fawned over the tiny bundle in her arms. Then, she shifted her gaze to Quinn's watery eyes.

Cameron whispered, "We did it. We brought him into this insanely awesome world."

Quinn gently brushed his thumb across Cameron's forehead, then leaned down to kiss her.

"And we'll protect him from it, always."

Outside the room, the team waited. After Cameron gave the okay, the med tech opened the door. Jeremy, holding hands with Kira, leaned against the wall. Axel impatiently paced, and Dr. Green fiddled with his newest invention, distracting himself.

"He looks just like his mom," Dr. Green said.

"I see a bit of grandpa in his face too," Cameron replied.

"So does this mean your son is a citizen of both multiverses? Which one are we in right now again?" Axel asked.

Everyone smiled. "That's a very good question," Dr. Green replied, and then he went off on a tangent like he usually did, weaving back and forth between theoretical physics and interdimensional politics before landing at baseball, which he often did.

Over the next several hours, a few teams made the rounds to visit the crew's newest member. Sentry even added the baby to his latest set of algorithms.

Hours turned into days, and the team wrapped up their studies of underground caverns and local inhabitants.

The new arrival combined with tech from two future multiverses inspired Dr Green and Sentry. In short order, they developed a portable shield to protect them from potential exotic particles.

Several days later, Quinn and the team prepared for their return from a subcommand room. "If it works as intended," Dr. Green explained, "we should be able to explore further into the multiverses without immediate threat."

Sentry added an explanation of how The Way modified different exotic particle variants to attempt the convergence and how the new shield technology would help them protect themselves and discover new places that might be in danger.

"I'm still trying to grasp the idea of one multiverse. I just hope we don't screw this up," Axel replied.

One evening later on the surface, the team gathered around a makeshift campfire. Axel raised a toast. "To new beginnings, to our tiny warrior, and to whatever the future holds."

The next day, they safely returned home.

Earth 2/Multiverse 1, planet surface, alternate Quinn's timeline, spring 2026

Alternate Quinn stared out the window of his expansive estate. The sun shone through a few thin clouds in an otherwise clear sky. Cameron rested on the bed, their newborn girl with her eyes closed and sound asleep in Cameron's arms.

A silver glint reflected the sun's rays and hinted at the work now underway to rebuild a new Tier 1, seeing as how the old one had been destroyed on their recent mission.

Quinn's team used the data from the future to speed up production by orders of magnitude. They only needed the raw materials. In just a day, they had built half of the device, with enhancements from tech half a century ahead. If the updates worked, future production times would decrease further, enabling near-instant construction.

Quinn broke his gaze from the stars and gently sat down next to Cameron, her eyes now open with the baby's. He smiled. "There you are," he said, briefly reflecting on his daughter's appearance fifty years in the future.

Quinn placed his finger in front of their infant girl. She gripped his finger tightly. "You're going to be fierce," Quinn said.

"And kind," Cameron added.

At their main base, the new baby symbolized hope. For alternate Quinn, seeing his infant daughter merged memories of her future self with the innocence she held now.

He'd now seen his daughter in multiple futures. They weren't perfect, and neither was his world. He knew no world or time ever would be, and he wouldn't want it any other way. Life without struggle would be empty and boring, but there was always room for improvement. They would still need to be diligent, both with their family and in protecting their world from the hidden forces that lurked in the background.

The events of the past few days, the chaos and the battles, faded. At that moment, it was about their little family. Quinn leaned in, pressing his forehead against Cameron's. They lowered their gaze toward their baby girl, her eyes wide open, examining her surroundings and trying to make sense of her new world.

Quinn let his eyes settle. Before long, he drifted to memories of his parents and mother when he switched minds with his father's body in 1984. His thoughts then wandered to what his parents' lives might have been like in the '60s. Thoughts of what he knew of that time drifted across the periphery of his mind, Kennedy, Dr. King, the moon landing, and then his mind went blank.

Quinn squirmed, shifting left and right until he rolled over and onto the floor. He awoke, but something tugging at the recesses of his mind told him not to open his eyes. He kept them closed and then reflected on something else.

Whatever happened, he didn't want to wake up in the '60s, and he wasn't even sure whose body he'd inhabit. He kept his lids closed and tried as hard as he could to think about something that had happened just the night before.

Quinn's thoughts raced between the first time he awoke in a time loop in Manhattan all the way to the supernova and then afterward. He drifted in and out of consciousness, ignoring the shifting noises outside his head, like a wheel of time spinning somewhere in the background. And then his thought went forward, reflecting on the times he'd seen the future.

The images of his progeny stuck with him. The future was inviting. He hoped by the time he arrived in real-time, it would remain that way.

If you enjoyed this book, please share and show your support by leaving a review.

Don't forget to visit the link below for your FREE copy of Salvation Ship.

https://royhuff.net/salvationship/

Printed in Great Britain
by Amazon